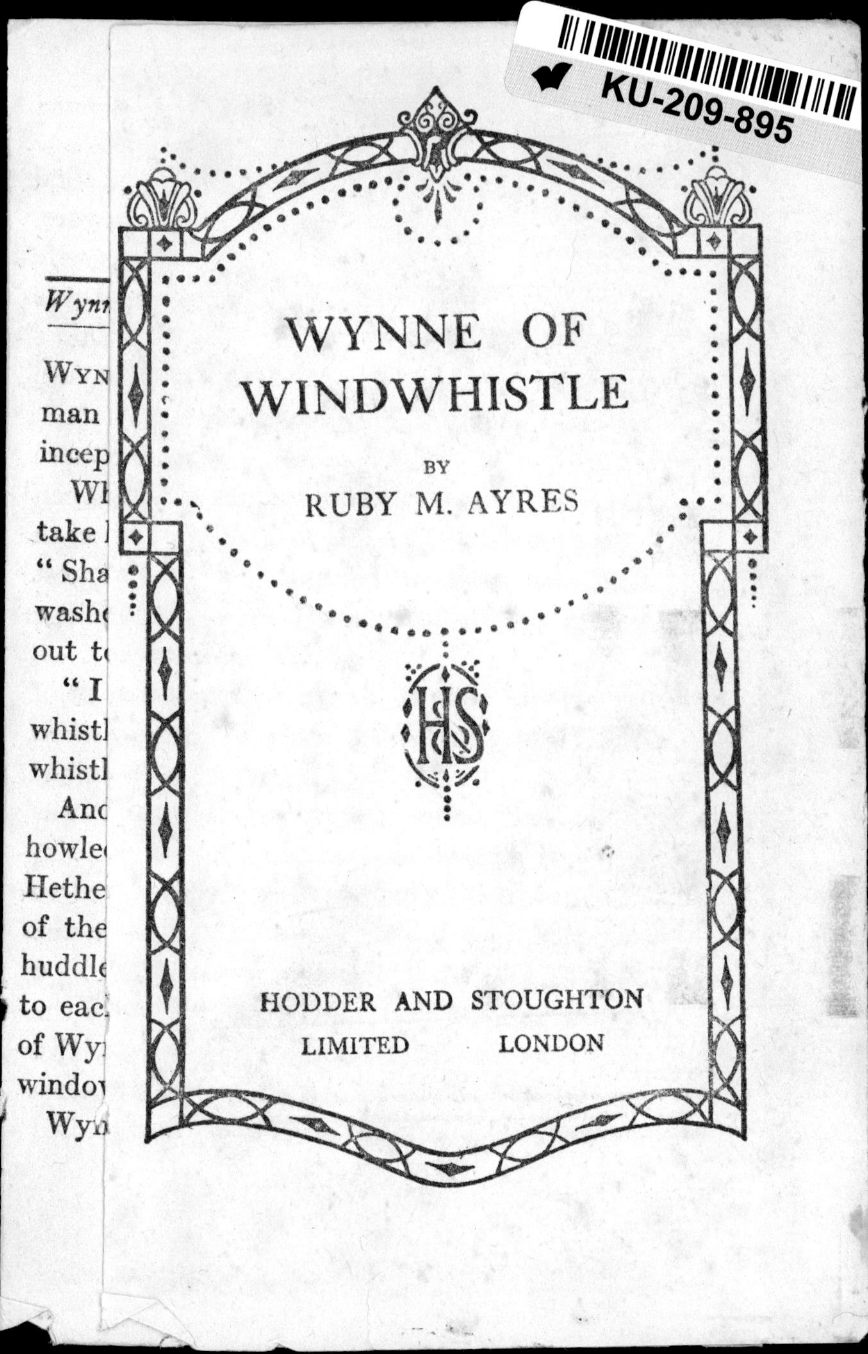

WYNNE OF WINDWHISTLE

BY

RUBY M. AYRES

HODDER AND STOUGHTON
LIMITED LONDON

He came of what the children's father called "A rotten stock," and he drank and swore, and—so it was whispered—knocked his wife about and bullied his only son who, so it was also whispered, had sworn to take his father's life the first time chance came his way and he was old enough not to bungle the job.

Windwhistle was a dilapidated old house which might, once upon a time, have been both beautiful and dignified, and it stood in solitary and frowning state on the highest of the many hills around the Surrey village of Whistlebarn.

It was a landmark from whatever point of vantage one looked, and one night, when the Hetherington children were about eight and twelve respectively, its old tower was struck by lightning during a violent thunderstorm, and the country people whispered to one another that it was the voice of the devil talking to Roger Wynne.

Whatever voice it was, the fright and the shock killed Roger Wynne's wife, and, two days later, she was buried with scant ceremony and what the children's father called "undue haste" in the moss-grown family vault which had not been opened for half a century; and Roger Wynne drank and swore more heavily than before, and his son, young Roger, grew more wild and unruly.

He was a big, loutish fellow of seventeen when Elspeth Hetherington first saw him, and he was engaged in the occupation of drowning a kitten in a weedgrown pond that stood in the corner of the neglected Windwhistle estate.

Elspeth had wandered into the grounds all unknowingly. She was a small child for her nine years, with a wistful, pretty face, and long, straight fair hair which she wore in heavy plaits over either shoulder; and seeing the big boy on the edge of the water, she walked up to him, all interest to know what he was doing.

She saw the kitten just as he sent it hurtling through the air, and she heard its last plaintive mew of fright and appeal as its soft little body struck the slimy water.

For the fraction of a second she stood paralysed, her eyes wide with tragic disbelief, then she screamed and rushed at young Wynne.

"You brute! You brute! You've murdered it!"

He swung round, staring at her from beneath frowning brows. Then he said sullenly:

"It was only a half-starved kitten."

"You brute! You brute!" she panted again, sobbing passionately. Then before he could guess her intention she turned and rushed into the water.

"You little fool!"

He caught and flung her back with a strong hand, and when she fell at his feet sobbing and beating the ground with both frenzied little hands, he said something which was a swear word only Elspeth did not know it, and, plunging into the pond, snatched the luckless kitten from death.

He waded back to the bank holding it at arm's length, and dropped it down beside the child with a contemptuous grunt.

"There you are! It's an ugly little brute, but if you want it——"

She looked up, her face white and distorted with grief, then with a startled cry she caught the kitten, wet and covered with weeds as it was, to her breast.

"Oh, thank you—thank you—thank you!" she sobbed.

Young Wynne laughed.

"Nothing to thank me for," he said ungraciously. "And stop howling. You look ugly when you howl."

Sheer amazement checked Elspeth's tears. Spoilt and sheltered as she had always been, no one had thought of telling her that she ever looked ugly, and her little face flushed as she stared at young Wynne with incredulous eyes.

A slow grin of delight crossed his face when he saw her amazement.

"Never been told that before, I suppose—eh?" he inquired.

"And I'm not ugly. I'm not!" she cried.

"Well, I say you are when you howl!" he retorted calmly.

She stamped her foot in its wet sodden shoe.

"You're a wicked liar!" she panted passionately. "And Wynne of Windwhistle will take you if you tell such wicked lies!"

"Wynne of Windwhistle!" He burst out laughing. "Who's Wynne of Windwhistle?"

Elspeth glanced furtively round as if fearful of being overheard.

"He's the devil, and he rides on the wind at night," she answered in a whisper, mindful of old Nanna's ghostly stories.

"Rides on the wind, does he!" The boy stared at her from beneath his beetling brows with a strange expression in his deep-set grey eyes. "What else does he do?" he asked curiously. Elspeth came a confidential step near, the draggled kitten still clinging to her.

"He used to knock his wife about," she whispered. "But she's dead, so now he knocks his son about instead."

Young Wynne took a threatening step forward.

"Who says he knocks me about?" he

demanded savagely. "I'd like to see him try! I'd kill him, I tell you! He doesn't dare lay a hand on me."

"Oh! Oh!" She was too frightened to run away; she just stood staring at him, blue eyes wide in her pale face. "Oh, who are you?" she asked tremblingly.

"I'm Roger Wynne!" he shouted at her, "and don't you let me hear you say again that my father knocks me about. He wouldn't dare. I'd kill him first!"

Elspeth closed her eyes in terror.

"I'll never say it again," she promised fervently.

"You'd better not," he threatened. "And get off our estate, that's another thing. You're trespassing, and my father shoots trespassers."

Elspeth did not need to be told twice. She ran as fast as her little legs could carry her over the rough, uneven ground, the kitten clasped in her arms, never stopping until she was safely out in the road again.

She was too terrified to tell anyone at home what had occurred. When they questioned

different man from its present owner; that he had had plenty of money, with which he had entertained royally; that the old house was always full of guests and the village people flourishing in consequence.

"Why is this one so different, then?" she asked wonderingly.

The doctor's mother, with whom she had been talking, lowered her voice, as most people did when speaking of the Wynnes.

"They say he's mad," she whispered. "They say that every other generation of Wynnes produces one madman. That's why he is never seen."

"I've seen his son, though," Elspeth said unthinkingly, then blushed. She knew it was nothing to be proud of that once she had talked with Roger Wynne. Mrs. Smithers shivered.

"A dreadful young man!" she said. "He will be worse than his father when he succeeds to the estate."

"I shouldn't think there will be much to succeed to, will there?" Elspeth asked, and she looked across the garden towards the hills where Windwhistle stood up against the sky like an ogre's castle.

Mrs. Smithers shook her head.

"He'll make money, or marry it," she prophesied. "That's what always happens in the family. One generation makes it for the next to lose, and so on."

"It's like a fairy story," Elspeth said dreamily.

"It's like a ghost story," Mrs. Smithers answered with energy. "I hate the Wynnes and Windwhistle. I wish it had been burnt to the ground the night it was struck by lightning." Her face cleared as the garden gate clicked and her son came across the lawn towards them.

He was a tall, thin man, with a grave face and rather sad eyes, and he had been in love with Elspeth ever since they were both small children.

He was the only doctor in Whistlebarn and for many miles round, and he worked from morning till night with but very small benefit to himself.

He did not know if Elspeth was aware that

he loved her, but he knew quite well that she did not love him, so he made the best of the friendship she had to give and tried to be grateful.

"Are you very busy, Ernest?" Elspeth asked. "You look so tired. Why don't you take a holiday?"

He smiled and shook his head.

"Holidays cost money."

"I wish he would go away for a rest," his mother said anxiously. "A holiday is cheaper than a long illness."

"But I can afford neither," her son reminded her. He looked at Elspeth, and his tired face grew more rested.

"It does me good to see you home again, anyway," he said.

"I am glad to be home, too," she answered. "Though it is rather quiet. Still, the country is lovely, and I've got the dogs." She glanced affectionately at the three animals lying at her feet and laughed. "They're not beautiful, are they, Ernest?"

They certainly were not, for all three were mongrels of the most impossible type, long-legged and shaggy, but all three had faithful, adoring eyes, and they loved the very ground on which their mistress trod.

"You have a good bodyguard, anyway!" Ernest said, laughing, and she answered:

"I should not be afraid to go anywhere if Shem, Ham, and Japhet were with me."

Mrs. Smithers laughed.

"What does the vicar say to your choice of names?"

"I don't think he minds," Elspeth said. "And I couldn't think of anything better."

She rose to her feet.

"Well, I must be going home." Her eyes wandered again to the tall hills, and the grey, forbidding walls of Windwhistle.

"You don't pay calls up there, I suppose, Ernest?" she said laughingly.

He followed the direction of her gaze.

"As a matter of fact, I did call there this morning," he said. "There were all sorts of rumours floating round yesterday. One of the Cocksedge boys swore that he heard the sound of a revolver shot and a lot of shouting, and there were certainly lights in one of the windows all night—a most unusual thing for the Wynnes. They generally seem to live in darkness. So I looked in this morning as I was going that way, and I saw young Roger. What a huge fellow he's grown, hasn't he ? "

" I've not seen him for years," Elspeth said, with a little reminiscent shiver.

" Well, he's a real giant in an ogre's castle now," Ernest told her. " I've never seen such a powerful-looking brute."

" And what did he say ? Was there anything the matter ? " his mother asked.

Her son shrugged his shoulders.

" If there was, he took good care not to let me know it. Never even asked me over the doorstep, and gave me to understand pretty plainly that I wasn't wanted."

" I'm sorry for him," Elspeth said.

Mrs. Smithers looked amazed.

" Sorry ! Why, he and his father are just wild beasts ! " she protested.

Elspeth made no reply, and they all turned to the gate, Shem, Ham and Japhet following at their heels.

" I'll call and see you one evening, if I

may," Ernest said diffidently when Elspeth said good-bye.

Her blue eyes met his serenely.

"Yes, do; we shall be pleased to see you." She laughed. "At any rate, I won't keep you waiting on the step as they did up there," she added, nodding towards Windwhistle.

She went off down the road, with the three dogs clamouring round her.

It was about six o'clock on an April evening, and although the sunshine was beginning to fade, it was still warm and bright enough to invite one to stay outdoors, so after a little hesitation, when she reached the corner of the road, Elspeth turned sharply to the right and away from home.

There was nothing particular to go home for. Her father would be shut up in his study, and dinner was not for another hour and a half.

And she loved being out of doors. As soon as she was well away from the village she took off her hat and walked along bareheaded, carrying it in her hand.

The dogs raced on a little way ahead, and

then came back to her, waving their odd, impossible tails, and looking up at her for approval with adoring eyes.

" Good boys ! " Elspeth said.

She loved them all, and declared she had no favourites, though perhaps there was a slightly warmer corner in her heart for Ham, whom she had found with a broken leg and bought from a village boy for two shillings.

" He ain't no use, miss. He'll have to be killed," the boy told her ; but Elspeth would not allow it.

She put Ham's leg into splints, and nursed him devotedly till he was well.

He would always be lame ; to the end of his life he would walk with a hop, skip, and a jump movement, but Elspeth loved him.

He was a bit of a collie about the head, and a bit of a sheep-dog about the body, and he had the oddest black spots on his legs.

" Ham, I believe your father must have been a rocking-horse," Elspeth told him solemnly one day when she was rebandaging the damaged limb, and Ham wagged his feathery tail as if to indicate approval.

"My dear, need you have quite such strange-looking dogs?" Elspeth's father asked hopelessly when the trio were first presented to him. "Surely you could have had a thoroughbred——"

"Thoroughbreds can always find homes," Elspeth said quickly. "My dogs can't! It's not everyone who would understand what darlings they are."

So she roamed the countryside with Shem, Ham, and Japhet, who would have torn to pieces anyone who dared lay hands on her, and was perfectly happy.

The dogs had turned into the woods now at the foot of the hill on which Windwhistle stood, and Elspeth followed. Primroses were nestling at the gnarled roots of the high old trees, and the footpath was soft and springy with moss.

The dogs went on ahead, snuffling at the warm earth, and Elspeth followed, stopping every now and then to pick primroses and bunch them together.

It was very quiet and deserted. There was no sound save the occasional twitter of a bird, or the flutter of wings. Once a brown rabbit ran across the footpath, and once a squirrel peered down through the branches where the little buds were swelling in readiness to show their leaves, but otherwise the woods were deserted.

Elspeth had gone some way before she realised, with a little start, that it was growing dark.

Outside the wood the sunset was fading fast, and inside the thickness of the undergrowth and trees overhead made it seem darker than it really was.

She stood still, whistling to the dogs, but they were out of sight. She whistled again, then called :

" Shem ! Japhet ! " And then, after a pause : " Ham, where are you, sir ? Come here ! "

But there was no reply, no eager scrambling through the brushwood to obey her call, and with a faint sense of surprise and alarm she ran forward. The footpath went upwards in a steep incline, which, as she knew, finally joined a wide, rough road which led direct to Windwhistle.

Elspeth seldom went far along that road; the old superstitions of her nursery days still remained in her heart, even if in a lesser degree, but to-day she forgot them in anxiety for the dogs, and she ran some distance without stopping till suddenly the silence was broken by Shem's shrill bark.

Elspeth called again, and he came running towards her, wagging his tail, but he would not stop, and ran back again almost at once down a side track leading to the left.

Elspeth followed. She was angry now; she meant to threaten the trio with the whip when she found them—a threat was as far as she ever got on the road to punishing them—when suddenly she came out into a little clearing made by some recently felled trees, and saw them all.

They were standing together on the edge of the clearing, as if not quite sure of themselves, and as if a little afraid of the man who sat on the fallen trunk of a tree, his head buried in his hands, paying no heed to them.

"Shem, Ham—come here at once!"

The man looked up at the sound of Elspeth's voice, and although it was eight years since she had been face to face with him, she knew him at once for Roger Wynne.

The hulking boy had grown into a man with—as Smithers had said—almost a giant's frame.

He was not bad looking, except that there was a hard, slightly brutal expression about his mouth and in his eyes, and when he saw Elspeth he said, without rising or giving her any sort of greeting:

"Call your cursed dogs off, will you?"

Elspeth flushed, and her heart began to beat quickly. She was not afraid, she kept telling herself that she was not at all afraid, and yet—all the old stories she had heard of this man and of his life, and Mrs. Smithers' recently spoken words came back to her with a rush.

"They say he's mad—they say that every

second generation of Wynnes produces a madman."

Supposing the idle gossip were true? And yet they were not mad eyes that looked so fiercely into hers, but only the eyes of one who knew a great and rebellious unhappiness.

And as she did not answer, he said again, angrily:

"Can't you hear? Call your dogs off."

Elspeth took a step forward. She had seen something now which turned her cold with fear, something which at the same time invested her with a new, strange courage.

When she was quite close to him, she held out her hand.

"Give me what you are hiding there," she said.

She saw the sudden start he gave, and her courage deepened.

"Give it to me at once!" she said again imperiously.

She was but a child in comparison with him, but now the fear in her heart was driven out by such pity that suddenly she bent and took the hand which he had thrust behind his back when first he heard her voice.

A big hand—a strong, firm hand—the hand which had once sent a helpless kitten to its death, and then snatched it back again in order to dry the tears of a child.

The memory went through Elspeth's mind in a flash as she stood there, her own small, trembling fingers holding his. Then, as if there were magic in her touch, the ugly, shining revolver which had lain in his grasp fell to the ground between them.

Elspeth drew a deep breath and stood back a pace.

"Only cowards do that," she said.

"I am a coward," Roger Wynne answered, and rose to his feet.

It was such an unexpected admission, such a pathetic admission, too, when one saw the height and strength of the man, that sudden tears welled into Elspeth's eyes.

"Oh, what is the matter?" she faltered.

His eyes were regarding her with rough suspicion.

"Who are you, anyway?" he demanded.

"My name is Elspeth Hetherington. Don't you remember me? You pulled a kitten out of a pond once because I cried."

"Was I fool enough for that?"

"I thought it was kind of you. I've liked you for it ever since."

"Liked me! The only soul on God's earth who does, then."

"Perhaps you won't let people like you," Elspeth said bravely.

"Let them!" He looked away from her into the heart of the darkening wood. "You'd better go," he said after a moment. "Why did you come this way at all?"

"I often come this way with the dogs."

"Dogs!" His grim face twisted into a dreary sort of smile. "A nice pack of mongrels they are!" he sneered.

"I know, but I love them," she answered.

"Lucky dogs!"

But he was sneering still, she knew.

"Well, you'd better go," he said once more.

"I will when you've told me why you—

what you wanted that for." She shivered as she looked at the little messenger of death lying on the mossy ground between them.

"Why do you want to know? It would have been all over if you'd stayed away another moment."

"Then I'm glad I came."

"Glad!" The sullen suspicion of his eyes was infinitely pathetic. It reminded Elspeth of a dog she had once seen in a French village—a stray dog who had never known kindness or care; a dog with which she had tried to make friends, but which had only slunk away from her showing its teeth in terrified apprehension.

But before she could speak he went on:

"You called me a liar last time we met, you remember? Well, now I can call you one for saying you were glad you came along in time to prevent me from blowing my brains out."

"It's not a lie, it's the truth. I am glad, and so will you be when you've had time to think things over," she insisted. "Whatever the matter may be, it can't be bad enough for that. Nothing is so bad but that there isn't some way of putting it right if you try."

"Preaching!" he said bitterly "But preaching won't help in this case."

He hesitated, his eyes on her face, then he said, speaking more quickly:

"I remember you because of your hair. You wore it in two long pigtail things, and it was fair like it is now—the colour of primroses——" He laughed as if in scorn at himself for remembering. "And you said that you'd been told my father knocked me about," he went on. "And I told you it was a lie, that he wouldn't dare, didn't I?"

"Yes."

"I said that if he laid a finger on me I'd kill him, didn't I?"

"Yes."

Roger Wynne laughed recklessly.

"Well, I believe I've kept my word. I believe I've done it!" he said defiantly.

"You mean—you mean that you've killed him?" Elspeth said slowly. And her face grew white.

She remembered what Ernest Smithers had told her not an hour ago, of shots heard up at Windwhistle and of lights all night in the windows, and her heart leapt in fear.

Roger Wynne saw the sudden blenching of her face, and he laughed.

"That frightens you, doesn't it? I thought it would. Well, I warned you to go. You only stayed to please yourself. Rather fancied the rôle of guardian angel, eh, till you found out you were dealing with a murderer?"

Elspeth shuddered.

"Don't say such dreadful things!" she implored. "I am sure, whatever has happened, it was an accident, of course. It must have been. You talk so wildly. I don't know if you are really serious or not."

He laughed again.

"Oh, I'm serious enough. The thing is what's to be done?" He glanced at the revolver lying between them. "That was the way I would have taken if you hadn't come interfering. But as it is——"

"As it is," Elspeth said, suddenly brave again "let me come up to Windwhistle with you and see what is the matter."

"You come to Windwhistle!" He stared at her incredulously. "Good heavens! What would people say?"

Elspeth flushed.

"What can they say? I only want to help. If anything is wrong, if your father is ill——"

"I tell you he's dead!" Roger Wynne interrupted ruthlessly. "I tell you he's dead, and that I killed him! The police are the people to be sent for. What's the good of a girl like you? You'd only scream or faint."

Elspeth stooped and picked up the revolver.

"I'm not a bit the screaming or fainting sort," she said quietly. "I'll come with you now if I can help in any way."

His dark eyes searched her with suspicion.

"You're not afraid?" he questioned gruffly.

She shook her head.

He pointed to the revolver.

"I suppose you think you could turn that thing on me if the occasion arose?"

"No; I'll give it back to you if you like. I know you won't be foolish any more."

His dark brows almost met in a scowl.

"If you think you've got me under your thumb——" he began.

Elspeth broke in gently.

"Aren't we rather wasting time?"

For a moment yet he stared at her undetermined. Then suddenly he shrugged his shoulders and turned.

"Come on then. It's a stiff climb."

He began to track upwards along the

narrow path, and Elspeth followed, the three dogs keeping close at her heels. They no longer showed any animosity to Roger Wynne. Anyone whom their mistress accepted was a friend.

It grew darker along the footpath as they climbed. The trees were very overgrown, and there was a tangle of undergrowth through which Roger ruthlessly trampled, leaving her to follow as best she might, until, flushed and breathless, they reached the top, which ended in a badly mended wooden gate and an unkempt garden beyond, which Elspeth knew was the beginning of Windwhistle.

There was a shadow of fear in her heart as she followed Roger Wynne through the gate and across the garden.

Nobody ever came to Windwhistle. There was a story that even the tradespeople left their goods at the corner of the road by the gate rather than go up to the house. It was probably only a story, but all her life Elspeth had only heard of Windwhistle as one hears of an ogre's castle in a fairy story, and even

with such implicit trust was really mad, as gossip declared ?

Supposing the story with which he had so played upon her sympathies was all fabrication, just to get her to follow him ?

For a moment she hesitated, and as if guessing her thought, Ham came closer to her and pushed his nose into her hand, as if to give her assurance

Elspeth's hand quickly caressed the dog's rough head.

She was safe enough, she told herself. Why be afraid ? And she went on, her own light step sounding like an echo of Roger Wynne's heavy feet as they crossed the stone-floored hall and he pushed open a door opposite. The room gave one a first impression of darkness and dustiness and of great age.

All the furniture was carved and unwieldly, looming up out of corners forbiddingly. A fire burned in a sullen smokiness on the wide hearth, and a man lay on a couch beside it, his bulky figure hunched uncomfortably beneath a torn rug.

Roger Wynne walked across the room and kicked the fire into a blaze with his foot, and Elspeth noticed how he avoided looking towards the couch with its silent figure. Then he spoke :

" There he is ! If you're afraid, go back and forget you ever came here."

" I'm not afraid," Elspeth answered, and wondered why she was not. The whole thing was so sinister and unusual ; and yet, in spite of everything, the deepest emotion in her heart was one of pity. In spite of his height and strength there was something of the overgrown schoolboy about Roger Wynne that appealed to her.

She seemed to understand his reluctant fear and his still more reluctant gratitude to her for what she was doing for him. She believed that he would like to have defied her and told her to go and leave him, but she believed also that the almost boyish dread of consequences in his heart forced him to allow her to remain, and even desired it.

Big man as he was, he was afraid, and because he was afraid he despised himself.

He kept his head averted as Elspeth crossed the firelit space and bent over the figure on the couch.

She could not remember ever having seen Wynne of Windwhistle before, but she felt that she would have known him anywhere as in the uncertain light from the logs she saw his face for the first time. A fine face, marred by a sternness of expression which amounted almost to brutality, marred by a looseness of flesh and a certain coarseness that seem to bear out all the vague gossip of him that had been whispered around the countryside for years. He lay with his head thrown uncomfortably back, and one long arm hanging over the side of the couch almost touching the floor, the hand of a giant at which Shem, Ham and Japhet sniffed suspiciously as one by one they cautiously approached.

Elspeth felt as if she were moving and acting in a dream as she gently moved aside the torn rug and laid her hand above the man's heart.

At first she could feel nothing, then slowly

she was conscious of a faint fluttering beneath her palm, and of a small, growing warmth. She turned round and looked at Roger.

"Have you any water—any brandy? How long has he been like this?"

"Last night—about midnight."

Her eyes indignantly accused him.

"And yet when Dr. Smithers came this morning you told him there was nothing wrong, and you would not let him come in."

"I hate Smithers. He only came out of curiosity. Besides I know there's nothing to be done. He's dead."

Elspeth went over to the window across which a heavy dusty curtain of some faded damask material was carelessly dragged.

She tugged at it in order to let in more light, and Roger watched her with suspicious eyes.

"What are you doing?"

"It's so dark. I want more light, and we want air, too." She turned on him angrily. "Don't stand there staring. Come and help me."

He obeyed without answering, opening the

rusty fastenings of the window and letting in the fresh evening air.

Elspeth gave a great sigh of relief.

" That's better. Is there anyone else in the house, or are you alone ? "

" Dorian is here somewhere about, and the girl."

" Please fetch them then, and some water, and then go for the doctor."

His face flushed angrily.

" I'll not have that fellow Smithers here. I told you——"

Elspeth met his sullen eyes quietly.

" Do you want your father to die ? " she asked.

His face changed inscrutably. He took a step towards her as if to speak, then he as suddenly changed his mind, and, turning round, strode out of the room, leaving her there listening to the sound of his heavy steps dying away across the stone floor of the hall. It was so like a dream. In spite of the open window and the rush of fresh air which beat into the room, Elspeth could not rid herself of the belief that none of the happenings of the past hour had been real. The spell of the mysterious was upon her, binding her hand and foot, and it was only by a supreme effort of will that presently she forced herself to stand again beside the couch with its motionless figure.

Wynne of Windwhistle had not moved, but when she timidly touched him once more, the faint movement beneath her hand seemed to be stronger and more definite, and she was wondering if it would not be possible to drag him closer to the open window when someone spoke beside her :

" Do you want water ? "

Elspeth turned with a quick, frightened breath to find a girl at her elbow.

She had entered the room quite noiselessly, and she carried a jug of water which she set down on a table while she stared at Elspeth, veiled animosity in her beautiful eyes.

" Do you want some water ? " she asked again. " Roger told me to bring some." And then, as Elspeth did not reply she added in a sort of whisper : " And what brought you here? We can do without people like you spying about."

Elspeth drew back a step.

"I came to help," she answered breathlessly. "I came because if I had not, Mr. Wynne would have killed himself."

The other girl laughed.

"You believe that? Pooh, he hasn't got the pluck to kill himself, no matter what he told you! Besides, why should he—and as for him——" She glanced contemptuously towards the silent figure on the couch. "It's a pity he didn't die years ago, and no tears to be shed either." There was such bitterness in her voice that Elspeth shivered.

"Who are you?" she asked.

"Who am I?" The girl laughed. "My name's Margaret Dorian, if it's of any interest. Heard of me?"

"No."

"Well, I live here. I was born here. My father has been with the family all his life, and his father before him, and we know just how rotten all the Wynnes are, and you'll know it, too, if you come here interfering again," she added coarsely.

Elspeth looked at her steadily.

Whatever else she might be Margaret Dorian was beautiful. Beautiful, perhaps, in a too full-blown, too common way, but her hair and eyes were magnificent, and her colouring reminded Elspeth of scarlet flowers she had once seen nodding in the sunshine against a white wall, or a Virginian creeper clad in its autumn tints. But her face was marred by its sullen look of suspicion, and without giving Elspeth time to speak, she said again:

"You take my advice and get away before Roger comes back. You take my advice and stop away, too. What made you come?"

"I've told you. I came to help. Mr. Wynne told me that he had accidentally shot his father."

"He told you—Roger told you that!"

For an instant the two girls looked at one another silently, then Margaret Dorian broke into loud laughter.

"He told you that, and you were green enough to believe it!" She stepped past Elspeth and laid a rough hand on the motionless figure on the couch. "Here, wake up!" she admonished him. "Wake up, and let's see if you're dead or alive."

Elspeth gave a stifled cry.

"You must be mad. You'll hurt him. Mr. Wynne has gone for the doctor."

"Hurt him!" Margaret's beautiful eyes met hers with a passion of scorn. "I'd like to hurt him," she said viciously. "I'd like to kill him if only I dared!" Then suddenly her manner changed, and she caught her breath with a frightened gasp, her eyes going past Elspeth to the doorway, the colour fading from her cheeks. Elspeth turned sharply round. She was afraid now, terribly afraid, though she hardly knew why, and she felt the blood draining from her heart as across the gloomy room she met the mocking eyes of Roger Wynne.

He was laughing, laughing as if something amused him very much indeed, and in a flash as she looked at him, Elspeth seemed to understand the trick that had been played upon her, and the trap into which she had walked.

Twice she tried to speak, but no words would come. She just stared at Roger, her eyes wide, her lips parted, and he laughed again as he said :

" Well, it was a case of ' " Will you walk into my parlour ? " said the spider to the fly, ' wasn't it ? "

" What do you mean ? " Try as she would, Elspeth could not keep her lips from trembling. " What do you mean ? " she asked again. She flung out one shaking hand towards the couch. " Isn't he—do you mean that you haven't hurt him, after all ? "

" Of course I haven't. Do you think I'm fool enough for that ? " Roger Wynne strode past her, and looked down at his father.

" He's drunk, that's all that's wrong with him," he said brutally.

" But you said—you said——" Elspeth faltered. She could hardly speak, and her voice died away, leaving her words unfinished, but he caught them up roughly.

"I said what I never thought you'd believe—but it served my purpose all right. I wanted to get you up here, and I've got you. I've seen you about the village, and I liked the look of you. I knew you'd never come here by fair means, so I got you by foul."

"You must be mad!" Elspeth whispered. She felt as if she were in a dream. Instinctively she backed away from him till she was against the wall, but he made no movement towards her, and for a moment the silence was unbroken.

Then Roger Wynne turned to Margaret Dorian.

"I don't want you. You can go."

At first it seemed as if the girl would have refused, then, with a shrug of her shoulders, she slipped past him and out of the room.

"Well," he said again to Elspeth, "you came readily enough when you thought there was a tragedy for you to pry into, and you came to please yourself, so now you can stay to please me."

"You must be mad," Elspeth said again.

He shrugged his wide shoulders.

"Perhaps I am. I know it's what they say about me. Anyway you're here, and here you're going to stay!"

She tried in vain to regain her courage; she even tried to laugh, but it was a little shivering sound that broke and died away.

"I've never done you any harm. It's cowardly to treat me like this. Please let me go."

"I never said you had done me any harm," he answered indifferently. "But you come from the crowd down below in the village that have frozen us out all our lives and shunned us as if we were lepers. I know what you've been taught about me and about my father. I haven't forgotten the way you looked at me years ago when I told you who I was—the day you made such a fuss about the kitten."

"You pretended not to remember me——"

"I remembered you all right. I always

meant to remember you. You're Elspeth Hetherington, and a month ago when your brother was home he had the cheek to ride across our land as a short cut to Whistlebarn!"

Elspeth cried out indignantly:

"Oh, I am sure he never did! And even if he did, how can I help it? Why need you insult me because of a thing you say he did a month ago?"

"I'm not insulting you. I'm just going to keep you here till you lose some of your airs and graces. I've had enough of being passed by you in the village with your nose in the air as if I were dirt——"

"But I've never even seen you! How can I have passed you?"

"I'm big enough to be seen, anyway!" he sneered.

There was a little silence. The room seemed to have grown darker, and glancing towards the window, Elspeth saw with sudden fear how rapidly the spring twilight was fading.

She tried to drag her courage together,

but she felt as if all will power had deserted her.

As if from a great distance she heard her own voice.

"I think we've had enough of this, Mr. Wynne. It's getting late, and I should like to go home. If you will walk down to the village with me——"

He only laughed.

"Holding a candle to the devil, eh? Thank you, but you're going to stay here."

He rose as if to come to her, and Elspeth cried out:

"If you touch me I will set the dogs on you!"

"Do you think that frightens me?" he asked. "But, as a matter of fact, I was not going to touch you. I was going to make up the fire."

He threw another log on to the smouldering ashes, stirring them into a blaze, and the leaping flames cast huge, tall shadows on the dark old room, making it, if anything, more sinister than before.

appealed strongly to her after the almost diffident gentleness of such men as Ernest Smithers.

Elspeth was young, and she had led such a quiet life that she had no experience to warn her, and the first rush of fear died down in her heart as she looked at young Wynne's triumphant face

With almost childish bravado she remembered the story of Claude Duval which she had read at school. Highwayman and rogue as he was supposed to have been, he had yet treated a fair lady with courtesy and consideration, and Elspeth had many times looked at the illustration to that story—of the crinolined lady and the befrilled highwayman dancing a minuet on the green—with a vague sense of envy and a faint regret that such days were no more.

And now here she was, high up in the decaying walls of Windwhistle, at the mercy of a man who, if he was not as attractive as the Claude Duval of the picture, was yet every bit as dominating a personality. And Elspeth remembered also that the crinolined lady of the coach had disarmed the highwayman with a kiss.

While her thoughts were hovering dangerously between fear and a strangely pleasant consciousness of the romantic, young Wynne spoke again :

" Well, have you got anything to say ? "

Elspeth found her voice with difficulty

" No, except that I am not at all afraid of you."

That seemed to nonplus him, and he moved a step nearer to her.

" You've no need to be afraid," he said. " I sha'n't hurt you. I am only going to keep you here."

" I sha'n't mind that," Elspeth said, but she put out a hand towards Shem, who had shuffled uneasily towards her.

Roger Wynne scowled. He hardly knew what he had expected—tears perhaps, or a scene—but this quiet acquiescence had not been in his reckoning.

It was true enough that he had brooded over the ostracism of his father and of himself; true that many times as a boy he had looked down at the village lying at the foot of the hill and angrily longed to be allowed to join in with other boys at football or cricket. But if fear of the Wynnes had been instilled into the hearts of Ernest Smithers and his friends, hatred of life and of his fellow-creatures had been the nourishment on which Roger Wynne had been reared from his cradle, until his vision and judgment had become so distorted that he could not see one fault in himself and could only lay the blame upon the rest of the world.

It was true that from time to time he had seen Elspeth about the village and had hated her for her innocent air of aloofness. Her fair daintiness appealed to his rough nature, and long before his encounter on the short-cut footpath with Bob Hetherington he had brooded over it bitterly, and wished for some means whereby he might humble what he considered to be her pride.

He had succeeded beyond his wildest dreams. When Elspeth followed him up the steep road to Windwhistle he had felt as proud as any chieftain of his capture, but now that pride was dimmed by her apparent fearlessness.

He would have liked tears and a scene; he would have liked her to be terrified; this calm acceptance of the situation did not fit into his scheme of things at all. After a moment he broke out roughly:

"If you're counting on the dogs——"

Elspeth laughed.

"Why should I count on them? I'm not afraid. You said you were not going to hurt me."

His wavering uncertainty gave her fresh assurance. Although in strength she was but a child compared with him, something seemed to tell her that she was mistress of the situation if she could only keep her nerve.

She put up her hand and took off her hat.

"I hope you don't mind," she apologised. "But I get such a headache if I keep my hat on for long."

She went nearer to the fire and sat down in a shabby armchair which was drawn up close beside it.

She was trembling a little and her hands were cold, and yet in her heart she was saying over and over again :

"I'm not afraid. I'm not at all afraid. They'll miss me soon at home, and then they'll send out and find me."

She dared not let herself remember that Windwhistle was the last spot for miles around where anyone would think of searching for her ; she dared not realise that she might have to stay in the deserted old house all night.

The man on the couch opposite stared, and flung up an arm, and in spite of herself Elspeth started and gave a smothered exclamation.

Young Wynne moved a step forward, standing between her and his father.

"He won't hurt you," he said quickly.

Elspeth gave him a grateful smile.

"I know. I'm not really afraid He only startled me"

She held out her hands to the warmth of the fire, then seeing how they trembled, she drew them back again, folding them tightly in her lap. There was a long silence.

It was quite dark outside now, and quite dark inside the big silent room, save for the light from the fire, which seemed to add to the weirdness and loneliness.

" What are you thinking about ? " demanded Roger Wynne suddenly.

Elspeth turned her eyes from the fire and looked up into his face.

" I was wondering what I have done to make you hate me enough to do this," she said.

She spoke very quietly, and with a little note of pathos in her voice.

" You see, I don't hate you," she added, as he did not answer. " I have often wondered why we could not be friends."

He laughed at that with a sullen sort of suspicion, then he said with apparent irrelevance :

" You called me a brute the day I flung that kitten in the pond."

" Did I ? Then I meant it. Any man is a brute who hurts an animal." She smiled

Elspeth felt a sudden desire to laugh. He was such a boy in spite of his giant body; such a boy in his alternate sullenness and gentleness that she felt almost old in comparison.

"You may come to tea with me to-morrow if you will," she answered very gently.

She felt his grip of her shoulders tighten.

"Is it true that you are to marry that fellow Smithers?" he dcmanded suddenly

"Marry Ernest Smithers?" Elspeth shook her head. "Of course it is not true," she said indignantly.

"He's not the man for you, anyway," he told her bluntly. "He's not a man at all. You'd despise him if you lived with him"

"He is the kindest man I know," Elspeth said defensively.

"Kind! Is that all you want?" Wynne sneered. "Any fool can be kind!"

"He is not a fool," she insisted quietly. "And he is a great friend of mine."

He flung away from her abruptly.

"Well, he won't be if he knows you have stayed here with me," he said brutally.

"I'm not going to stay," she answered with quiet confidence. "You are going to take me home. I should be afraid to walk all the way down that path in the dark alone, but if you come with me I sha'n't mind——"

He looked at her irresolutely.

"Is this just your cunning way of trying to manage me?" he demanded. "If it is——"

Elspeth interrupted him.

"Do you never think anything nice of anyone?" she asked.

She heard his quick breathing.

"I could think all the nice things in the world of you," he said roughly. "But I don't believe in you. You look at me as if you—as if you mean what you say, but you can't! I'm a hulking great fellow—you must be frightened of me."

"Why must I be? You said you wouldn't hurt me." She started as a hollow-toned clock boomed somewhere in the house. "It startled me," she explained hurriedly, her voice shaking.

She wondered how much longer she would be able to keep her self-control; she wondered frantically if they had yet missed her at home.

She so often went for long walks with the dogs, she so often stayed out till long after dark. Why should they be anxious to-night? Sudden trembling seized her, and her whole body shook so that she could hardly stand. Every nerve seemed strained to snapping point, and it was only by an almost superhuman effort of will that she kept herself from crying out in terror:

"Let me go—let me go——"

Then Roger Wynne came back to where she stood.

"If you mean what you say—what you've said," he broke out—"if you're not trying to make a fool of me just to get away, kiss me and I'll take you home."

Elspeth did not move, she felt as if she had suddenly been turned to stone.

In all her life she had never kissed a man, except Bob and her father. As a child she had always shrunk from playing games wherein kissing was considered part of the fun. In the queer little romantic niche in her mind which sheltered Claude Duval and all the other black sheep of the story-books, was stored also a little secret vow that she would never kiss any man until the Prince Charming who was to outride all others should come into her life.

And now this man—this Wynne of Windwhistle—of whom she had never heard any good, but only evil, was calmly offering to put an end to this torturous scene for the price of a kiss.

She looked up at him with blind eyes. The dark room with its blotches of red firelight seemed to be swimming round her. She wondered in terror if she could be going to faint. She clenched her hands till the nails cut into her soft palms. Then slowly the mists cleared away and she saw Roger Wynne's face above her, not sullen any more, nor brutal, but just a little strained and wistful, with something of the unhappy boy in its expression that touched her heart with a feeling of pity.

She tried to speak, but her voice seemed to have gone, and she just lifted her face and kissed him, as he had asked, very gently.

She drew back, trembling and waiting, and the seconds throbbed away like hours before either of them moved or spoke.

The Roger Wynne said in a voice quite changed: "I'll take you home now."

Elspeth caught her breath in a gasp of agonised relief. She had had no real hope of his sincerity, and although she did not know what she had feared, fear had been in her heart.

The relief was almost more than she could bear. She wanted to cry, the tears seemed to be surging up in her throat, choking her, and she could only just find voice enough to whisper one word:

"Thank you."

He led the way across the room and Elspeth followed with the dogs at her heels eagerly excited and anxious to be gone. There was a dim lamp burning in the big hall outside, and by its light Elspeth saw the girl Margaret Dorian standing at the foot of the big staircase looking after them.

She called to Roger sharply:

"Where are you going?"

He glanced at her over his shoulder.

"Down to Whistlebarn."

The girl said something else which Elspeth could not catch, but Roger made no reply. He dragged open the heavy front door, holding it for her to pass out, then he let it fall back heavily into its place.

It was very dark outside, and Elspeth stood still.

"I can't see. It's so dark," she faltered. Then she felt his hand on her arm.

"I know every step of the way. You need not be frightened." He kept his hand on her as they went forward, and after a moment he said again, with something of his old suspicion: "You do not say now that you are not frightened."

Elspeth tried to answer him, tried to force a laugh, but it was beyond her, and suddenly the tears came, and uncontrollable

She did not want him. Now she was safely down in the village again with its lighted streets and sense of security, a full realisation of what had happened seemed to come home to her with a feeling of horror.

She looked up to where she knew Windwhistle towered above them in the darkness.

Supposing he had kept her there all night? The very thought made her shake, but before she had time to speak Roger said again:

"I suppose you'll tell everyone what a blackguard I've been."

And Elspeth answered:

"You've not been a blackguard, and anyway I shall never tell anyone."

He gave vent to a little harsh exclamation.

"Do you mean that?"

"Of course I do"

He groped through the darkness and found her hand

"I don't know what to say to you. I want to say heaps of things and I can't." His voice almost sounded as if he were angry with her, and the grip of his hand hurt.

She interrupted gently :

" Say them to-morrow when you come to tea."

" You really mean that I may come ? "

" I shall expect you at four o'clock."

He released her hand and turned away without answering, and Elspeth stood where he left her, staring after him down the dark road.

" It's a dream. Of course, it's just a dream," she told herself again dazedly when at last she began to walk on.

A dream that she had ever been within the walls of Windwhistle ; a dream that she had ever kissed Roger Wynne—kissed him !

A wave of revulsion swept through her heart.

How could she have done such a thing, how could she !

She broke into a little run as if to outstrip the memory of what had happened. To have kissed such a man ! Now that the danger was past, she felt ashamed to the depths of her soul.

And to-morrow he was coming to tea.

the separation from him which first school, and afterwards business, had necessitated.

"But why are you here?" she demanded again breathlessly, and then as she saw the frown between his eyes she hastened to add for the third time: "Oh, I am pleased to see you"

Bob growled.

"Well, it's more than the guv'nor is," he said sullenly. "I got anything but the fatted calf from him, I can tell you." His eyes searched his sister's face with vague suspicion before he went on bluntly: "The fact is I'm fired."

"Fired!"

"Yes." He shrugged his shoulders impatiently. "Don't look so blank," he grumbled. "And for heaven's sake close your mouth. It doesn't suit you to have it wide open. I'm fired! Chucked out, pushed off, or whatever you like to call it."

Elspeth shut the side door, which she had left open behind her in her surprise, and took off her hat, pushing back her hair with a bewildered feeling.

"Who's pushed you off?" she asked faintly. "I know I'm stupid, but I don't understand"

He explained sullenly.

"The firm, I mean, stupid! Old Blythe and Barrow. Narrow-minded old fools. And all because I've backed a few horses."

Elspeth's cheeks flamed.

"You mean they've—sacked you?" she gasped.

He frowned again with a sort of nervous irritation.

"They can't sack me, because I was never paid," he answered. "But they told me they preferred my room to my company, and they're going to return half the guv'nor's premium." He laughed mirthlessly. "Nice thing, isn't it?"

Elspeth put out trembling hands and clutched him by both arms.

"Bob! You haven't done anything—wrong!" she whispered.

He wriggled away from her.

"I told you. I'd backed a few horses, and lost. You're just like the guv'nor.

He barked up the same tree. Thought at once I'd gone off with the petty cash, or falsified the books or something."

Elspeth gave a sigh of relief.

"I never thought any such thing," she declared.

"Sounded rather like it, all the same," her brother said curtly. "Here, let's get something to eat. What time are we supposed to have a meal? And why are you so late?"

The memory of the past two hours came back to Elspeth with a rush, and now it seemed more like a dream than before, now it seemed more impossible still that it could ever have happened.

"I'll tell you while we have supper," she said huriedly. "Wait while I get tidy. Supper ought to be ready."

She ran up to her room, tidied her hair, washed, and came down again breathlessly.

Supper was ready, and Bob was already at the table.

"Guv'nor not coming?" he asked.

Elspeth shook her head.

"He hardly ever does. I send all his meals to his room."

Her brother's eyes softened as they rested on her.

"Bit dull for you, eh?" he asked.

"Sometimes," Elspeth admitted with a sigh.

She served the meal and sat down to table.

"I'll give you a dozen guesses, and you'll never find out where I've been," she said after a moment.

Bob was not particularly interested, he found his own thoughts all engrossing for the moment.

"Round at Smithers', I should think," he said negligently.

"No."

"Tea at the vicarage?" he hazarded.

"No."

"Can't guess, then—and pass the bread, please."

Elspeth obeyed, and was silent for a moment before she launched her bombshell.

"I've been up at Windwhistle."

Bob looked up sharply.

"Up at Windwhistle! Rubbish!" he protested.

"It's true. I've been in the house"—she shivered. "Oh, that horrible house! I should think it's haunted by evil things. It's so dark and neglected."

Bob went on with his food.

"You dreamt it," he said flatly. "You couldn't get into Windwhistle if you tried for twenty years. Nobody ever goes there, you know that."

"Well, I've been, anyway," Elspeth insisted quietly. "I got in quite easily, thanks to you."

"Thanks to me!" He stared at her blankly. "My good child, you must be delirious," he protested. "What on earth have I got to do with it? I haven't been near the place for years."

Elspeth broke in quickly:

"You rode over their short cut road last time you were home! It's no use denying it. Roger Wynne told me about it himself."

"Roger Wynne told you!" Bob burst

out laughing. "Put your hand out and see if you're still in bed," he mocked her.

But Elspeth did not laugh. She was conscious of a sudden strange feeling of discomfort, as if she had been found out in telling a senseless lie. She leaned her arms on the table and stared across at her brother.

"Are you speaking the truth?" she demanded.

"The truth? Of course I am. What do I want to tell a lie for? I haven't spoken to Roger Wynne for years. I hate the fellow. I wouldn't speak to him whatever happened. He's a perfect outsider, and everyone knows it."

Elspeth flushed crimson, remembering the last few hours.

"Will you swear—will you swear on your word of honour," she said earnestly, "that you didn't ride through the Windwhistle short cut, and that you haven't seen Roger Wynne for—well, this summer?"

"It's the truth if I never speak again," her brother insisted. "Though what on earth you're driving at I can't imagine."

Elspeth sat up with a little sigh.

"I'll tell you," she said.

Bob listened very quietly, his eyes fixed on her face. Though he was careless and happy-go-lucky in many ways, he yet had a great respect and affection for his sister, and it made his blood boil to think of the indignities to which she had been subjected. And by a Wynne, of all people! A Wynne, despised by the whole village and shunned even by the working people, had dared to kiss her! He started up, his face crimson.

"The beast! I'll pay him out for it. I'll thrash him within an inch of his life."

Elspeth laughed shakily.

"You couldn't," she answered. "He's three times as big as you are. He's a giant! That's partly why I was so afraid. I believe he could have broken me with one hand."

Bob was pacing up and down the room, his hands thrust into his pockets, his eyes full of fire.

"I'll make him pay," he said again excitedly. "If I have to wait half a lifetime I'll make him pay. Have you told the guv'nor ?" he demanded abruptly, swinging round.

"Of course not! Do we ever tell him anything?" Elspeth asked rather scornfully.

She was fond of her father, but she had a sort of contempt for him. What was the use of being a man, she often asked herself, if one could not be strong, and assert one's authority.

Mr. Hetherington had never asserted his authority. He was a mild, easy-going man, entirely wrapped up in himself, and all he asked of life was to be let alone, and to be allowed to absorb his identity in his own interests.

He was fond of his children in a detached sort of way, and gave them everything as far as his means would allow; but beyond that he took no interest in them, and never inquired how they spent their time. Neither of them would ever dream of going to him if they were in trouble, and if they had done so he would have been utterly at a loss to know how to help or advise.

And the thought came to Elspeth as she sat watching her brother pace up and down the room so agitatedly, that she had made a mistake in telling him about Roger Wynne, and that she would have been wiser to have kept it to herself.

The old tradition that no Wynne could possibly be of any good was not necessarily a true one, she knew, and against her better judgment she found herself remembering that there had been moments up there in the grim old house when she had almost liked young Roger, and had at any rate softened towards him.

She broke out into hurried excuse and defence

"I was to blame, too, of course. A great deal of it must have been my fault. I should not have gone there. But I really thought it was genuine. You see——" she broke off helplessly.

"Girls are so gullible," Bob said scornfully. "I suppose Wynne's good-looking, or something about him appealed to you."

"Nothing about him appealed to me at

all," Elspeth answered indignantly. "I only went because I was sorry for him, and I only did what I did, and told him he could come to tea to-morrow, because there was nothing else to do. After all, he might have kept me there all night if he had wished to."

"If he had I'd have shot him."

She laughed a little at that.

"Anyway, there is no harm done," she insisted. She pushed back her chair and rose. "Let's forget it. I'm going to."

"Forget it? When he is coming to tea to-morrow." He regarded her with suspicious eyes. "Have you told me all the truth?" he demanded.

"Bob, of course I have!"

He turned to the door.

"Well, when he comes I shall be here to give him his tea," he said darkly. "And you can keep out of the way."

"Perhaps he won't come after all," Elspeth said hopefully.

Her brother laughed.

"Oh, he'll come all right," he prophesied.

It rained hard the following morning.

alone. I'm busy. Nobody ever seems to think that my work is of any importance. You must see him for me, Elspeth, and find out what he wants. Tell him I am ill—tell him anything you like, only keep him away from me."

"But, father——"

For once Mr. Hetherington asserted himself.

"You'll do as I say. When Barrow comes, you will see him for me. You're quite capable of dealing with him."

"But I've never seen him in my life! And after all his business is with you"

"He's quite a decent fellow. You'll get on well with him. Run away now and don't argue. I've got a lot of work before me."

Elspeth obeyed. She knew it was useless to try to argue with her father when he was in this mood. For a mild man he could be curiously obstinate when he chose. But she shrank from interviewing George Barrow. She had heard a lot about him from her brother, and did not like what she had heard. Barrow was a rich man and a bachelor.

"He think's he's bought the earth," was Bob's way of putting it. "He got his position on his father's money, and not on any merit of his own. I hate the fellow."

So Elspeth was fully prepared to hate him also, and there was unconscious antagonism in her manner when she went down to the drawing-room later on in the day where he waited for her.

He was standing by the window when she entered, and he turned round and began to speak, then stopped, looking at her questioningly.

"Miss Hetherington?" he asked.

"Yes." Elspeth did not offer to shake hands, and for a moment they looked at one another with antagonistic eyes, then Barrow said hesitatingly:

"It was your father I wished to see."

"I know, but father's ill." She stumbled a little over the words. "He hardly ever sees people, Mr. Barrow, so he asked me if to tell her. " I'd give my right hand—and even now it's not too late. Things can be hushed up."

From a great way off she heard her own voice.

" You mean he's taken money that was not his." And then Barrow's reluctant admission :

" Yes, I deeply regret. I'd give anything to have kept it from you, but my partner—you see, it was not possible."

In spite of a certain loneliness, there had never been any great trouble or unhappiness in the life of Elspeth Hetherington, but as she stood helplessly staring at George Barrow's pained face, words which an old nurse of hers had once spoken in long ago nursery days came crowding back to her memory.

" It's all right to be happy and free from care, but trouble comes. We all get it sooner or later."

Elspeth had thought it rather a foolish remark at the time—she saw no reason, for instance, why trouble need ever knock at her own door. And yet now here it had come with a resounding crash.

In spite of his assertion to the contrary, Bob had done something terrible—something so terrible that the knowledge for the moment stunned her, and left her incapable of either feeling or consecutive thought. She had heard of men who took money which did not belong to them, and she knew that such things were punished by terms of imprisonment, but that Bob, her own adored brother, should ever be guilty of such an action was past belief. And yet at the back of her mind was the bitter consciousness that she was not altogether surprised. Bob had always been extravagant, and never fond of work. She remembered, with a terrified feeling, that once, years ago, she had caught him taking money from a little box in which she had been laboriously saving her pennies in order to buy a Persian kitten. He had laughed at her at the time.

" I was only borrowing it," he declared contemptuously. " I should have paid you

He told himself that, at all events, the girl was innocent, and it seemed a horrible thing that she should be made to suffer. And while he hesitated, seeking for words, she asked again:

"Does it mean—will he have to go to prison?"

Barrow impulsively held out his hand and took hers.

"There must be ways of getting round the trouble," he said, with unwonted gentleness. "I am more sorry than I can say, and if there is anything I can do to help——"

Tears rose to her eyes and brimmed over.

"Is it—very much money?" she faltered.

He looked away as he answered her.

"I'm afraid so—nearly a thousand pounds."

She gave a stifled cry.

"A thousand pounds! Oh, he must have been mad! And he told me—he told me—oh, can you lose so much money on horses?" she asked childishly.

The ghost of a smile crossed Barrow's face.

"Very easily, I am afraid," he answered. He did not like to tell her that horses were not the only way in which Bob had gambled, and, afraid that she would question him further, he went on quickly: "But I think matters can be easily arranged if the money is repaid. My uncle—Mr. Blythe is my uncle—can be persuaded to hush the whole affair up if the money can be repaid."

"And how do you think we can get the money?" Elspeth asked hopelessly. "Bob and I haven't got a thousand shillings between us."

George Barrow fidgeted.

"There is your father—surely he will help——"

Elspeth laughed.

"Father hasn't got the money, either, I am sure, and if he had he would never pay it out for Bob. He's like that. Although he's such an easy man in some ways, he can be hard when he likes, and he would never lift a finger to help. He would sooner let Bob go to prison."

"If you will allow me to see your father——"

"Oh no, no!" She moved between Barrow and the door, as if afraid that he would insist "Oh no, no!" she said again earnestly. "He simply mustn't know—at least, not yet. Let me see what I can do first. There must be some way out, there must!"

"It's not fair that you should have the worry and the responsibility," Barrow said angrily. "I wish to heaven I had not come. It's unpardonable that you should be placed in such a position."

She tried to smile.

"Oh, I don't mind at all! I love Bob, and I would do anything to help him. Mr. Barrow, will you promise me not to do anything for a day or two—not to tell father, I mean—or to let Mr. Blythe do anything, till I have had time to try what I can do?"

He promised readily enough, although he had no belief that she would be able to avert the disgrace.

"Though what on earth I can do I don't know," she told herself frantically, as she watched him walk away down the road. She wrung her hands. "Oh, what can I do!"

Bob had not come back, and in the meantime she tried to think of some story with which to satisfy her father.

"What did Barrow want?" he demanded, without much interest, when she went back to his room. "If it's any complaint against Bob I don't want to hear it. The firm's probably to blame, anyway, I've got no time to be bothered."

Elspeth looked at him with indignant eyes.

"I suppose it's of no interest to you to know what Bob is to do in the future, then?" she asked hotly.

Mr. Hetherington frowned.

"He's had his chance, and if he chooses to let it go that's his fault," he said gruffly. "I've no money to waste on him. Let him go abroad and shift for himself."

"Mr. Barrow wanted to see you, and I

said you were ill," Elspeth said in a stifled voice.

"So I am ill," her father retorted. "At least, I shall be if I'm worried to death by you children."

Elspeth walked out of the room.

Although she was relieved by her father's attitude, yet it made her own helplessness seem more acute. What was she to do—to whom could she turn?

Bob came in at lunch-time. She heard him slam the front door and cross the hall whistling as if he had not a care in the world, and her heart failed her. Was he really so indifferent to what he had done? How did he imagine things were going to be settled? When she heard him go into the drawing-room she followed.

He had thrown himself down in a big chair by the fire, his legs stuck out to its warmth, and was settling down to read a racing paper. Elspeth went forward and stood beside him.

"Mr. Barrow has been here."

She saw the little start her brother gave,

but for a moment he made no reply, then he gave a short laugh.

"The deuce he has!" And then presently: "Did he—did the guv'nor see him?"

"No; I did."

There was an eloquent silence, then Bob sat up, casting his paper on to the floor.

"Well, what did he tell you?" he asked defiantly.

"Everything!"

He glanced up into his sister's white face, then rose to his feet with an impatient exclamation.

"It's no use preaching," he said sullenly. "The thing's done. If I hadn't been unlucky, nobody would ever have known. Other chaps do what I've done and get away with it." He began to pace up and down the room excitedly. "There never was such cursed bad luck as mine. Everything I touch goes wrong. It's uncanny. If I'd only had one decent win I could have pulled round. I could have pulled round as it is if they hadn't found out. Old Blythe is a beast! He's as rich as Crœsus, and yet for the sake of a few paltry pounds——"

"A thousand pounds is a lot of money, Bob."

He turned on her angrily.

"Not to him—it's nothing to him. He'd never miss it. He doesn't know what it's like to have nothing but a few shillings to spend, and to have to work like the dickens for that. It's enough to make a chap dishonest, to have nothing himself, and to see so much all round him."

Elspeth said nothing. She felt as if she were seeing her brother for the first time in her life, or else that he had changed so terribly since yesterday that she did not recognise him at all. Her silence seemed to anger him, for he stopped and looked at her with sullen eyes.

"What's he going to do, anyway?" he demanded. "I suppose you agreed with him that I'm the worst kind of blackguard? I suppose you let him say all sorts of things about me——"

"He was very kind. He's given us two

days in which to find the money and pay back the firm."

Bob laughed.

"Good heavens—what a hope! Two days—he might as well give us two hundred years, or two minutes—it's all the same!"

She caught at his arm with trembling fingers.

"Bob, there must—there must be some way!"

He shrugged his shoulders.

"Do you know anyone with a thousand pounds? I don't! And if we did, do you think they'd let us have it? Not that I want them to," he added, with bravado. "I don't care a curse if they do send me to prison!"

"Don't say such things—don't say such things!"

"What else can I say? I'm guilty all right, and I'll take the punishment!"

"If they send you to prison I shall die!"

"Don't be a little fool." He squeezed her hand and let it go. "It's not your fault, Elspeth. Nobody can blame you.

There's a black sheep in every family." He paced away and stood looking down into the fire. "I suppose, of course, it would be useless to tell the guv'nor, and see if he'd lend a hand?" he submitted gruffly, after a moment.

Elspeth shook her head.

"I don't believe he's got the money, and even if he had——" She could not go on.

"Well, that's that, then," Bob said laconically. "It's no use worrying. I'm not the first chap who's gone to quod, and I sha'n't be the last."

Elspeth burst out crying.

"How can you say such things? Aren't you ashamed or must I be ashamed for you? Oh, Bob, what is the matter with you? I thought you were so different! Can't you help me think of some way out? Don't we know anyone to help us?"

"No millionaires," Bob answered dryly. He looked white and drawn, and a great deal of his indifference was assumed, although in spite of what he had done he was no coward, and now the worst had come to the worst he was fully prepared to pay the price. "Unless Smithers is any use?" he added.

Elspeth dried her eyes, but the tears came again.

"Ernest has no money, you know he hasn't," she said reproachfully. "And even if he had—how could I ask him?"

"Well, he's sweet on you. I should have thought it was a good enough reason."

She did not say that it was the very reason why she could not ask help of Ernest Smithers. She had nothing to give him in return and never would have.

Bob picked up his racing paper.

"Well, is there any reason why we can't have lunch?" he asked carelessly.

Elspeth ran from the room sobbing.

"What is the matter with him that he can feel no disgrace?" she asked herself wildly. What was the matter with him that he could calmly admit to being a felon, and not realise the shame of it?

She stayed in her room till she saw him

leave the house again, then she put on her hat and coat and went out.

She was at her wits' end to know what to do, or to whom to turn, and she had forgotten all about Roger Wynne and the fact that he was supposed to be coming to tea until, when she reached the road, she saw his tall figure coming towards her. She would have turned back to avoid him had there been time, for her face was red and disfigured with crying, and she was in no mood to talk to this man of all people, but he had seen her and had already quickened his steps.

"Coming to meet me?" he asked eagerly as he came up to her.

"Coming to meet you!" Elspeth repeated his question indignantly. "Of course I was not coming to meet you! As a matter of fact, I'd forgotten all about you," she added deliberately.

"Oh!" He looked down at her from his superior height, a queer sort of expression in his eyes, then he asked abruptly: "What's the matter?"

"Nothing!"

" Is that why you've been crying so that you can hardly see ? " he demanded uncompromisingly.

She made no answer, and after a moment he said :

" I'll come with you if you're going for a walk."

" I'm not."

" Well, I'll come with you wherever you are going," he insisted imperturbably, and as she moved on he walked beside her.

She turned her head away to hide her quivering lips and the tears in her eyes. In the last twenty-four hours life seemed to have been wrenched out of its ordinary easy rut, and to have torn her away with it.

They walked some way silently, till Wynne asked again with a touch of anger :

" Why can't you tell me what's the matter ? I thought we were going to be friends."

" I don't want to be friends with you or anyone," Elspeth broke out passionately. " I think life is horrible and everyone in it."

"That's a pity," he said soberly. "Because since yesterday I've been thinking it's not so bad after all, and this morning something else happened that made it seem better still."

"I'm glad somebody is cheerful," Elspeth said bitterly. "I'm glad everyone isn't a liar and a—thief——" she bit the last word back before it was half uttered, but he heard.

"Meaning me?" Roger Wynne asked, his dark face flushed. "I've been called a great many things," he went on after a moment, "but I've never yet deserved to be called a thief."

"Or a liar?" Elspeth asked.

He hesitated.

"I told you a lie yesterday," he admitted, presently. "I told you several lies, and I'm sorry."

She laughed mirthlessly.

"You need not be. It makes no difference—and, anyway, I know all about it now. Bob told me."

"Your brother?"

"Yes. He told me you had made it all up; that he had not seen you for months, and that he had never ridden over the Windwhistle short cut, as you said he had."

They had turned off the main road on to a field path, which was wind-swept and deserted, and there was nobody to see when with sudden impulse Roger Wynne laid his hands on Elspeth's shoulders.

"Look here," he said roughly, "I dare say you'll laugh at me—I quite expect you will—but do you know what I'm going to ask you?"

She shook her head, the tears still tumbling down her face, and yet at the back of her mind she was conscious of an odd sort of contentment because of his grasp of her shoulders, and even because of the rough sincerity of his voice.

"I'm going to ask you to marry me," said Roger Wynne. And then there was a long silence, during which they stared at one another, she in blank disbelief, and he with a sort of fierce defiance. Then he said:

"Well, hasn't any man ever asked you to marry him before?"

"Yes, but"—her tears had dried as if by magic—"but I don't know you. I've only spoken to you twice in my life until to-day. Besides——"

"Besides, you don't even like me, you mean," he interrupted. "Well, I don't expect you to. You haven't had a fair chance yet. But I can make you if I want. I get most things I want in this world if I set my heart on it hard enough."

She shivered a little, remembering last night up at Windwhistle and the way in which this man had looked at her across the big dreary room that had seemed so strangely haunted.

He went on, not giving her time to speak.

"I'm not in love with you, don't think I am, but I want to marry you all the same. There's something about you——" He broke off, to resume again after a moment. "There's another reason, too—the thing that happened this morning. We've had some money left to us." He laughed.

"That's a thing that hasn't happened to a Wynne of Windwhistle for a couple of centuries, but the luck has turned at last. No, it's not an uncle from Australia, or anything you read about in story-books. It's an old friend of my father's—someone I've never seen. Made his money dishonestly, I believe—moneylending or floating shady concerns; anyway, he made it, and we heard this morning that he died a month ago on his way out to China, and that everything is left to us."

He paused, but Elspeth said nothing; she just looked at him with her tear-drenched eyes.

"Don't you like money?" he asked, half laughingly, half in irritation. "It's all most women think about."

It was all Elspeth was thinking about at the moment; her world seemed bounded to the north, south, east, and west by the sum of a thousand pounds.

Roger Wynne went on:

"It's quite a lot of money, too; we don't know how much yet, but enough to do up

Windwhistle and put the family fortunes on their feet again." He shook her in his impatience. "Well, haven't you anything to say? Will you marry me and come to live up at Windwhistle?"

Elspeth closed her eyes. In her distress it seemed as if this man had fallen clean out of heaven to help her; she forgot everything but that the way by which she could save Bob was here, and that she had only to stretch out her hand to make sure of it.

There was nobody else for whom she cared. The only man who had ever wished to marry her was Ernest Smithers, and she was quite indifferent to him. Poor Ernest, who had been such a faithful friend!

She raised her eyes to Roger Wynne's dark face above her. He looked very much in earnest, she thought, he looked—almost as a man in love might look—even though he had said that he did not love her!

And then she forgot everything except her own distress and need, and she broke out tremulously:

"If I marry you—oh, I know it sounds

dreadful!—but if I marry you, will you give me a thousand pounds?"

"A thousand pounds!" She saw the subtle eagerness die out of his face; felt his grip of her shoulders relax; then suddenly he laughed.

"A thousand pounds! Is that your price?" He pulled her to him with ungentle fingers. "Well, I suppose you're worth it," he said cynically, and, bending, kissed her lips.

WHEN Roger released Elspeth from his arms he stood back with a little laugh and looked at her with hard eyes.

"Well, I suppose it will be worth a thousand pounds," he said again bluntly.

He was rather flushed, and his lips when they touched hers had seemed to burn.

Elspeth wondered if she would ever forget that kiss. There had been something so brutal about it. It had been less like a lover's kiss than that of a man who, having bought a thing and paid a high price for it, considers he may use it as he pleases.

There was nothing gentle about Roger Wynne. He was much more of a cave man than the perfect lover of whom Elspeth, like all other girls, at one time had dreamed.

She knew that she was trembling as she stood there, a little faint and shaken, looking helplessly at him.

Dream upon dream seemed to have been crowded upon her during the last two days, and this one was no more real than the rest had seemed. Soon, she was sure, she would wake up and find that none of it all had happened; that she had never spoken with Roger Wynne, nor been told that her brother was a criminal; that she had never set foot in Windwhistle, nor felt a stranger's kiss upon her lips. And yet she had just promised to marry a stranger—in exchange for a thousand pounds. It sounded absurd!

She looked round the bleak field and up at the grey, rainy-looking sky with a feeling of unreality.

How could she marry this man? It was a sheer impossibility! And yet she had promised. And Roger Wynne was not a man who would allow a promise to be lightly broken.

"And may I ask what you want the thousand pounds for?" Wynne broke in upon her thoughts mockingly, his dark eyes fixed upon her tremulous face. "Or isn't it part of the bargain that I shall be told?"

"It wouldn't interest you," Elspeth said. She put out a timid hand and touched his arm. "Oh, I hope we shall be good friends!" she appealed.

His face softened.

"I'll play the game if you will," he answered rather gruffly.

They looked at one another in silence. Then Elspeth said:

"Well, I suppose I must get back home."

"Shall I come with you and tell your father?" Roger asked.

She gave a little exclamation of dismay.

"Tell father? Oh, no!"

"He'll have to be told some time or another."

"Yes, but there is no hurry, is there?" she asked tremulously. "There is plenty of time."

He frowned.

"You mean—— Do you imagine I am going to be engaged to you for months?"

She made no answer, and he went on:

"I assure you I am not. I am not a patient man. When I want a thing, I want it quickly. A special licence is good enough for me. I'm going to London to-morrow to get one."

She cried out in dismay.

"But I can't marry you like that! What will people think?"

"I'm afraid it has never troubled me what people think," Roger Wynne answered hardily. "No doubt they will say all sorts of rotten things, the people in this one-eyed village always do." He regarded her with suspicion. "Is that what you are afraid of? Ashamed of me, I suppose."

She raised her head proudly.

"If I were ashamed of you I would not marry you."

"I'm not too sure of that," he answered.

He turned, and they began to retrace their steps across the field to the road.

"I'd better come and see your father and make sure," he said again after a moment. "I'm not afraid of him, if you are."

"I'm not afraid of him for myself," she told him quickly. "But—oh, well, you wouldn't understand."

"You can explain, can't you?"

She shook her head. She did not know whether to laugh or cry. This was surely the strangest courtship she had ever heard of.

It seemed impossible that she had just promised to marry a man who was not even troubling to be polite to her, a man whose very name she had always feared and dreaded.

She could imagine what her father would say. He would say that she was mad. He would first of all get very angry, and then he would stop arguing and shut himself up in his laboratory and refuse to be bothered any more.

There would be no help to be had from him; no advice or sympathy. Even if she told him the truth about Bob he would be unmoved, she knew. He would say that Bob had made his own bed and must lie on it. When they were almost within sight of the house she stood still and looked at the man beside her.

"Please don't come any farther," she begged.

"Why not?" His dark face set in obstinate lines. "Look here," he said roughly, "if you're playing a game with me, trying to make a fool of me——" He broke off. "I'm sorry," he admitted grudgingly after a moment, "but I don't understand you. Why are you willing to marry me, anyway?"

She cast about in her mind for a reply. Obviously she could not tell him the truth and say "For a thousand pounds." And yet surely he must guess that there was no other reason? Surely he could not imagine she was in the least attracted by him?

Before she could find an answer he asked another question:

"What about that fellow Smithers, and all the other men you know? Surely some of them must have wanted you? I can't be the only one who——"

He stopped.

"I don't care for men," Elspeth said a little haughtily. "And if there was anyone I liked better than I like you I should not have promised to marry you."

He flushed.

"Does that mean that you do like me a little?" he asked haltingly.

Elspeth did not answer. She could not truthfully say that she did. And yet there was something appealing about him at that moment that made her hesitate to hurt him.

"If you will be straight with me," she said impulsively, "if you will be honest with me, I will be with you, and then everything will be all right."

"Who says I'm not honest?" he demanded.

She flushed as she met his angry eyes.

"You were not very honest yesterday," she reminded him.

"I'm no worse than that brother of yours!" was his quick retort. And then, as he saw the bitter chagrin in her eyes, he hastened to add: "I'm sorry. That was caddish. I'll never say a thing like that again. And now let me come and see your father."

"Oh, please—no!"

"Why not? He must be told."

She cast swiftly in her mind for some way of evasion. What was the use of telling her father? Even if he was sufficiently interested to try to prevent the marriage she knew she would not allow him to do so. She had made up her mind to go through with it whatever happened.

"Can't we tell him after we are married?" she appealed at last, in desperation.

"You mean you are willing to marry me at once?" he asked incredulously.

Elspeth flushed painfully.

"You said—I thought you said you would get a special licence," she faltered. "And if so, we can be married any time, can't we? I don't know much about such things, but——"

He caught her hand.

"Come to London with me to-morrow, and we'll be married at once." His voice was quick and eager. "We've nothing to wait for." He laughed excitedly. "Heavens, what will people say?"

Elspeth did not particularly care what people said. She was too young and too distressed for her brother's sake to realise what a terrible blunder she was making. She did not see that she was walking blindfold towards the edge of a precipice. She only saw herself as the saviour of her brother in disgrace.

"Very well, I'll go with you to-morrow," she said quietly.

But Roger Wynne was still suspicious.

"You're playing the game? You're not deceiving me for some scheme of your own?"

She looked at him silently, and he apologised with almost boyish haste.

"No, I know you're not. All right, to-morrow, then. Will the ten-thirty train do? It gets up in three hours."

"Yes."

"You'll meet me at the station?"

"Yes."

"All right."

He had turned away when she called to him.

"Mr. Wynne."

He looked back.

"I've got a Christian name," he said hardily, "and if we're to be married so soon you might as well call me by it."

"Very well. Roger, then." It spoke eloquently of her indifference to him that she could use his name without the least embarrassment. "I only wanted to ask——I mean, when could I have the money?"

"Money? Oh,"—his face changed grimly—"that thousand pounds, you mean!" He hesitated. "I dare say I could get it advanced. When do you want it?"

"Oh, at once, please!" she urged earnestly. "If I could have it to-morrow—"

"Cash down—eh?" he muttered. "All right. We'll see."

He strode off down the road, and Elspeth went back home.

She felt as if she were walking down the road of a nightmare city, and yet she was far more excited than afraid.

How people would talk! She could imagine the dismay and gossip that would run through the village when the news became known.

"Elspeth Hetherington has married Roger Wynne."

Nobody would believe it. Not even the greatest scandalmonger in the village would credit such a story. And yet it would be true. She laughed hysterically to herself as she slipped up to her room and took off her hat.

What a courtship! No engagement-ring--no happy days with the man she was to marry. Just a strange bargain driven, and then a hurried marriage in a registrar's office.

Like most girls Elspeth had had her own thoughts of a wedding—of a white frock and many flowers and bridesmaids, of a wonderful honeymoon and happiness ever after—and instead she was to take this dark, strange man for her husband, and go to live with him up at Windwhistle.

With a sudden feeling of superstition, she

"You're just in time for tea. How cold your hands are!"

"I've been out all day, and the wind is keen."

He spoke nervously, and he looked nervous. He sat down on the edge of a chair and rubbed his hands together.

"Sugar?" Elspeth asked.

"Two, please."

She gave him his tea, and a little silence followed.

"Are you very busy, Ernest?" she asked presently.

"I am rather."

He seemed to find conversation difficult. He stirred his tea, and then set it down and left it to grow cold.

"I want to ask you something," he said at last bluntly.

Elspeth looked up in surprise.

"Ask me something?"

"Yes. May I?"

"Of course. What is it?"

He fidgeted, rubbed his hands again, and

rose to his feet as if he felt at a greater advantage.

"I dare say you'll be angry," he appealed helplessly, "but I've got to ask you. It's all over the village, or I wouldn't bother; but as it is—— Elspeth, were you up at Windwhistle last night?"

His kind face grew very red as he asked his question, and his eyes were full of a distressed apology.

"I hate to ask you," he said again. "And in my heart I know it's not true. I know it couldn't be. And yet—I had to ask you."

Elspeth sat with her hands folded in her lap, dumbly staring up at him. Her heart was beating jerkily and her lips felt dry.

"Of course I know it isn't true," Ernest said again, pleadingly. "But I had to ask you. I had to get a denial from you yourself before I tell the people who are talking that it's a lie."

Elspeth tried to speak but no words would come. It gave her a sense of anger to see through this man what everyone thought of Windwhistle and those who lived there. In the past few hours she had forgotten that until yesterday her own thoughts had been identical with them. And as she hesitated, uncertain what to answer, Ernest said again:

"Of course, you're angry. You've every right to be angry. I know what you've always thought of the Wynnes. I can't imagine how such a story started."

"How did it start?" Elspeth asked.

And now there was a little secret amusement in her heart How startled the village would be! What a nine-days' scandal it would give them.

Ernest shook his head.

"One of the maids from the vicarage said she saw you coming down from Windwhistle late last evening with Roger Wynne. She said—forgive me, my dear—that you and he were arm-in-arm. It made my blood boil when the story came to me. Then this afternoon I heard it again from three different people—in a more exaggerated form, I am sorry to say. It's abominable how such lies get about."

"They're not lies," Elspeth said.

"Not lies!"

He stared at her incredulously. Then he smiled a little nervous smile.

"You're teasing me," he protested. "I know that, of course. I know——"

"I'm telling you the truth," Elspeth said quietly. She had risen to her feet also now, and was standing close beside him. "I was up at Windwhistle last night, and I did walk down with Roger Wynne. His father was ill. At least——" She broke off, remembering that even her sympathy for the old man had been gained by a trick.

"Don't look so angry, Ernest. After all, the Wynnes are no worse than anyone else in the village——"

"No worse!" He stared at her in bewilderment. "Elspeth, what are you saying? Everyone knows what the Wynnes are."

She tossed her head disdainfully.

"Oh, I don't believe half the stories!"

"You don't believe them!" he echoed.

"No!" She met his eyes angrily. "And I don't see what right you have to come here and cross-question me!" she broke out. "They are all scandal mongers in this village."

"Elspeth!"

"So they are!" she insisted. "And if you listen to them you are just as bad! Anyway, I don't want to hear what they say! Roger Wynne was very nice to me, and I like him!"

It was not really the truth, but she felt driven to defend the man whose wife she was so soon to be.

After all, what did the village people know of him or of Windwhistle? None of them had ever been inside the old house; certainly not half a dozen of them had ever spoken to Roger.

But she was sorry when she saw the pallor of Ernest's kind face and felt his hands relax their hold of her, and her anger swiftly died.

"Don't let us quarrel, anyway," she said quickly.

"I don't want to quarrel with you,"

he answered stiffly. "You know I think more of you than of anyone in the world. I——" Suddenly his stiffness deserted him, and there was a passion of eloquence in his voice as he broke out: "You know I love you! You know I've always loved you! You must know that I should have asked you to marry me long enough ago if I'd had anything to offer you! But you're worth someone so much better! I could make you happy, I know! Elspeth——"

And then, as if his long-imposed self-restraint had broken down at last, he went on hoarsely:

"Marry me, my dear! I'll be so good to you! I love you so much!"

She tried to stop him, and failed. She did not want his eloquence. Although with Roger Wynne she had missed everything of which she had ever dreamed, somehow his bluntness had appealed to her more strongly than this man's pleading.

"Oh, stop, Ernest—please, please!" She freed herself gently from him and moved away, her eyes full of tears, her breath coming fast. "I don't love you! I never could—not in that way! I like you very much, but——" She hesitated. Then, seeing the pain in his face, she told him the truth. "There is someone else I have promised to marry."

LIFE had not been kind to Ernest Smithers. As a boy he had never been able to have the advantages other boys of his own age took for granted, and as a man he had had to work hard in order to help keep his mother He had kept his love for Elspeth suppressed, always fully realising how little he would have to offer her, but to-day his self-control had deserted him, only to fling yet another disappointment in his face. After the first pang he took it without flinching. It was no more than he had always expected. He had never been conceited enough to imagine that she could care for him.

He turned away for a moment and stood staring down into the fire with blank eyes. Then he found his voice :

"Well, I hope you will be very happy, whoever the lucky man is," he said, with an effort.

"Thank you, Ernest."

There was a little silence. He had not asked who the man was, and Elspeth wondered why. She did not understand that at the moment Ernest's sole concern was with his own bitterness. He had lost her, and that was the only thought for which there was room in his heart.

Presently he turned round and looked at her.

"I hope you will be very happy," he said again.

Elspeth flushed and the tears rose to her eyes.

"I'm sorry—so sorry!" she stammered. "I like you so much. I do wish—I do wish——"

"Don't blame yourself." He gave a faint smile. "I never really thought you could care for me, but—well, hope dies hard, you know." And he went away without a backward look.

Elspeth found the tears running down her cheeks, and she wiped them away, with a little ashamed feeling. After all, she was not to blame, but she did wish she had told Ernest about Roger Wynne.

Now the first excitement was over, she began to feel a little lonely and apprehensive, It was all very well to read in books of romantic girls who ran away and got married without anyone knowing about it, but in this case things seemed different. She knew so little of Roger Wynne. How did she know that all her life she would not regret the rash step she was taking ?

Then she remembered for whose sake she was doing this thing, and her courage returned. She loved her brother so much, and they had always been everything to one another. How could she stand by and see him disgraced ? She comforted herself with the thought that after to-morrow everything would be all right, and that Bob's safety would be assured. After all, it mattered very little about herself.

When Bob came in later for his tea she greeted him as if nothing had happened ; but he stood in the doorway, looking round with a scowl.

"Hasn't he come?" he demanded blankly.

"Hasn't who come?" Elspeth asked.

"Wynne. You said he was coming to tea."

"Oh!" She felt her colour rising. "Well, he hasn't come yet," she said evasively.

"Did you put him off?" he demanded, with suspicion.

She shook her head. She would have given a great deal had it been possible to confide in her brother, but she was afraid to do so. He was in a quarrelsome mood, she could see, and she thought she understood him well enough to know that he would never tolerate the thought of her marriage with Roger Wynne even in order to save himself.

Bob sat down by the fire and stuck out his long legs, staring gloomily at his boots.

"Seen the guv'nor?" he asked abruptly.

"Not again—no."

Bob laughed without much mirth.

"Wonder what he'll say when he hears I've been hiked off to gaol?" he said cynically.

Elspeth shivered.

"Don't say such things! Something will turn up—I am sure it will," she said quickly.

He stared at her with morose eyes.

"What sort of thing? The end of the world?" he asked, with dreary sarcasm.

"Something will turn up," she insisted positively. "Something always does when things look blackest."

"You're an optimist!" he sneered. He rose to his feet, pushing away the cup of tea she had put on the table beside him. "I don't want it! I hate tea!" he said irritably.

Elspeth followed him as he turned to the door, and caught his arm.

"Don't worry, Bob," she said very gently. "Things will be all right. I know they will."

She did not see him again that evening, although late that night, when she lay awake, unable to sleep for restless excitement, she heard him creep upstairs to his room. He was miserable, she knew, and afraid. Yes, that was the word—afraid. She did not like to apply it to her brother; it was the sort of word one should not have cause to apply to any man, she told herself. And yet she knew it applied to Bob. He was not brave enough to face the trouble he had brought upon himself. She wished that to-morrow would come more quickly.

In the morning it rained heavily. Elspeth was conscious of terrible foreboding as she dressed herself with hands that were not quite steady. The sun might have shone for her, she thought, and she remembered the little saying: "Happy is the bride the sun shines on." Was this an ill omen for her, that the skies were so grey and unbroken and the rain poured down so steadily?

As she went down to breakfast she stopped outside her brother's door and knocked. There was no answer, and she tried the handle.

"Bob!"

No answer still, and, thinking he was asleep she went on downstairs. She was used to having her meals alone, but this morning her loneliness seemed almost more than she could bear. In an hour or two she was going to be married, but nobody knew.

There would be nobody to wish her good luck or to speed her on her way. All she had to look forward to was a journey to London with a man of whom she was still more than half afraid, and then—what?

"It's for Bob! It's for Bob, and he's all that matters!" she told herself feverishly.

She made a poor pretence of eating her breakfast, then went up to her father's room. But Mr. Hetherington was tired and did not want to be disturbed.

"It's not often I stay in bed," he complained. "Surely I can be allowed a little extra sleep sometimes?"

Elspeth stood at the foot of the bed, looking at him pleadingly. If only she had dared to tell him! If only he had been like other fathers!

"Well, what are you waiting for?" he asked querulously. "Haven't I told you that I don't want to be disturbed?"

"I only want to tell you that I am going to London by the eleven train," his daughter answered, with an effort.

It was not very often that she went to

London, and she expected a storm of questions and criticism, but Mr. Hetherington only closed his eyes.

"Well, run away," was all he vouchsafed.

Elspeth checked a desire to laugh. He little knew that it was exactly what she was going to do, she told herself as she went to her room and put on her hat and coat.

There were the three dogs to take for a run first. She wondered whether Roger Wynne would object to having Shem, Ham, and Japhet up at Windwhistle. He had called them mongrels. She remembered that with resentment. Perhaps he would not allow her to have them when she went to her new home.

"I shall do as I like," she told herself determinedly, as she hurried downstairs and out into the yard where the three dogs were kept.

They greeted her with a chorus of delighted barks, and, when she let them off their chains, raced round her, pawing at her feet.

"They may be mongrels," Elspeth told

herself defensively, " but they're perfect darlings and I love them."

She took them for a walk through the fields and back along the high road. She tried to keep her thoughts from Windwhistle and the foolhardy marriage which was drawing so near, but it was difficult. Whichever way she looked, the grim walls of Windwhistle seemed to confront her; however hard she tried to control her thoughts, they kept harking back to Roger Wynne and his fierce eyes.

" I shall be able to manage him," she told herself with a confidence which she did not really feel.

As she turned back home the village church clock struck the half-hour. Elspeth hurried her steps, Ham keeping close to her heels.

She took the three dogs round to the yard again, but Ham refused to be chained up. Usually the most obedient of the three, to-day he kept some distance away, and whenever Elspeth approached him he ran off, whining restlessly.

"I believe he knows what is going to happen," she told herself and her apprehension grew. In the end she caught him and chained him to his kennel, dropping a remorseful kiss on his rough head before she turned away. She heard him whining still when she entered the house and ran upstairs, hurriedly changing her hat and coat.

"I suppose I must wear my best," she told herself, tremblingly.

She asked the maid if Bob had come down yet.

"I don't think so, miss. I knocked at his door but there was no answer. Shall I try again?"

"Oh, no," Elspeth said hurriedly. "Don't bother. Just tell him I have gone to London if he asks."

She was afraid of seeing Bob before she left—afraid lest she might break down and tell him what she was going to do.

She had to run to catch her train, and she arrived at the station breathless and flushed, to find Roger Wynne already pacing up and down, his dark brows scowling above his eyes.

"I thought you weren't coming," he said ungraciously when she joined him.

Elspeth stood still, breathing fast.

"I always keep my word," she answered resentfully.

"Oh, do you?" he said gloomily. "Well, I've got the tickets, and the train is just going."

It was hardly a happy beginning. Elspeth felt inclined to cry as she followed him along the platform to a first-class carriage.

They sat opposite to one another, the rain beating against the windows.

"Did you tell your people?" Roger Wynne asked abruptly.

She shook her head

"I thought we agreed not to," she faltered.

"I never knew a woman who kept her word yet," was his only answer.

Elspeth bit her lip. This was worse than she had anticipated. If the train had not already been swiftly moving she would have got out and left him ; but it was impossible. She clasped her hands hard together to hide her trembling. Presently she spoke, trying desperately to be cheerful.

"We're not going to quarrel, are we ? It's such a bad beginning, to quarrel on our wedding-day."

She felt as if she were talking nonsense. How could this be her wedding-day ? How could this disagreeable-looking man, with the scowling brows, be her future husband. The frown lifted a little from Roger's eyes.

"I thought you were going to let me down," he half apologised. "I've been let down so often in my life, I don't like it."

She forced a smile to her trembling lips.

"Well, I haven't let you down, you see, and I never shall. I told you yesterday that I would be all right to you if you are all right to me ; I thought we made that a bargain."

"I suppose we did," he admitted reluctantly.

After a moment he leaned over and caught her hand, holding it hard.

"Do you like me at all?" he asked tensely.

She was trembling from head to foot, but she answered steadily enough:

"I like you very much when you don't scowl at me and frighten me to death."

He laughed at that and his face cleared, making him look years younger.

"We shall get on all right," he prophesied almost happily.

He felt in his coat pocket.

"I've got that cheque," he said abruptly. "I've kept my word, you see; I've kept my word to let you have it before we're married."

"You're very kind," Elspeth said gratefully, and tears of sheer thankfulness filled her eyes. "I think you are very kind," she said again.

He flushed and looked embarrassed.

"Hope you'll always think so," he said gruffly.

He relapsed into silence after that, pretending to read a newspaper; but he glanced at her from behind its pages from time to time. Elspeth sat very still, watching the pouring rain.

" If only the sun would shine," she kept telling herself desolately. " If only the sun would shine just for a few minutes."

But the sun refused to show itself. London was drenched in rain when they arrived, and the streets were muddy and horrible.

" We'll have a taxi," Roger said.

He strode out of the station ahead of her, and Elspeth followed him through the crowd as quickly as she could.

" He's going to make a funny sort of husband," she told herself with an hysterical desire to laugh, and, for no reason at all, she thought suddenly of Ernest Smithers—kind Ernest, who did not think the world good enough for her.

She dragged her thoughts away from him with an effort, afraid because suddenly her heart was warm towards him.

Roger Wynne had called a taxicab and had opened the door.

" Let's get out of this cursed rain," he

said irritably, and took her arm to hurry her.

They drove away through the pouring rain in silence.

Elspeth's thoughts were all now with her brother. Somehow or other she must get that cheque to George Barrow before they left London—only then could she feel secure.

Twice she tried to broach the subject to the man beside her, but each time her courage failed. Suddenly Roger spoke, with a grim sort of mirth.

"Not much of a wedding-day, is it?"

She forced a smile to her lips.

"Never mind. The rain doesn't really matter, does it?" she said bravely.

"Doesn't it?" He shrugged his shoulders. "I suppose you're trying to make out that we love one another so much, and are so happy together, that nothing matters. Is that it?"

Elspeth flushed sensitively.

"You are not very kind," she protested.

"I hate humbug," was his uncompromising reply.

She looked away from him, biting her lips to keep back the passionate words that rose to them.

After a moment she asked:

"Where are we going?"

"To get married," he answered bluntly.

"Oh!"

She felt herself trembling again. There was no escape now, she knew. She had got to go through with this thing that was becoming more of a nightmare with each passing moment.

Was she going to be a coward at the eleventh hour and let her brother down? With an effort she forced herself to speak.

"I think the rain is stopping a little."

Roger leaned forward and rubbed his sleeve over the window-pane.

"You don't have to make conversation with me," he said rudely. "And, if anything, the rain is worse than it was."

He let the window down with a bang.

"Here we are!" he added.

The next hour was like a dream. The bareness of the registrar's office, the registrar's cold, disinterested face, the scratch of his pen as he filled in the certificates, and the monotonous sound of the pouring rain on the grimy windows.

There was a pale-faced clerk at a corner table who kept coughing in a hollow, unreal sort of way and glancing apologetically at Elspeth after each spasm.

Then Roger's voice :

" You sign your name here, Elspeth."

How her hand shook as she obeyed ! There was a mistiness before her eyes.

" I can't see properly," she faltered.

Roger's big figure seemed to fill the room. To Elspeth's overstrung imagination he seemed like a giant waiting to carry her away, a prisoner for life, to his castle up in the mountains.

Then it was all over, and the registrar was speaking again, offering her his hand.

" That is all. May I congratulate you both and wish you every happiness ? "

She heard Roger laugh.

" Oh, thanks ! " he said dryly.

She tried to say something herself, but no

words would come. And a moment later they were out in the drenched street, where the taxicab waited at the kerbstone.

A shabby woman in oozing shoes and a soaked shawl came up to them and thrust a bunch of violets into Roger's face.

"Buy them for the lady, sir. No luck without flowers on your wedding-day, you know!"

She was evidently used to the customs of the registrar's office.

Elspeth expected Roger to refuse, but to her surprise he stopped, chose half a dozen sweet-scented bunches from the basket the woman hid under her shawl, and thrust a ten-shilling note into her hand.

"I've no change, sir," she faltered. "It's the first lot I've sold to-day."

"I don't want any change," Roger answered. He took Elspeth's arm. "You're getting wet through. Get in," he said in a domineering tone.

He followed her into the taxicab and told the driver to take them to the Savoy.

Elspeth shrank back into a corner, and for

the first time a full realisation of what had happened came home to her. She was married. This man was her husband. She glanced at him from under her lashes. What was he thinking about ? she wondered nervously. As if feeling her regard, he turned and laid the violets on her lap, putting an arm strongly round her.

"Well, you're my wife now," he said jerkily. "So I suppose I may kiss you as much as I like, eh ?"

He did not wait for her to answer. He crushed her to him, his lips seeking hers.

Elspeth gave a little, startled cry, half of fear, half of anger. She had never been handled so roughly before, and she was conscious chiefly of bitter resentment.

Then she remembered Bob. It was for his sake she was here at all ; for his sake she was bound to put up with Roger Wynne's domination.

But for a moment she managed to hold him in check.

"You're not playing fair," she said breathlessly, trying to laugh. "Kisses cost money!"

How she hated having to say such a thing! It sounded so cheap and artificial.

Roger Wynne drew back offendedly.

"What do you mean?" he demanded.

Elspeth looked him steadily in the eyes.

"Only—I haven't had my thousand pounds," she said. "Give me that first, and then I will kiss you."

Although Elspeth tried to speak lightly, there was a feeling of tragedy in her heart.

She did not want to kiss Roger Wynne, and she did not want him to kiss her.

Her heart was fluttering like a wild thing and her body felt as cold as ice. Though loose, the very new wedding-ring on her finger seemed to cut into her flesh, a significant reminder, and through her brain a monotonous voice seemed to be saying again and again:

"You no longer belong to yourself. This man has bought *you*. You no longer belong to yourself."

She felt the grip of his arms relax from about her, and saw the eagerness of his face change to its old sulky look once more. She was sorry then that she had repulsed him. Perhaps it would have been wiser to have submitted first to his kisses and then to have reminded him of his promise.

But Elspeth had no experience of men. As a young girl she had been singularly shy with those who would willingly have paid her attention, and she was too nervous now to realise the extreme tact which her present situation required.

There was a little silence, then Roger Wynne drew away from her, to say sullenly :

" I don't want kisses I have to pay for." Elspeth's colour rose, and her heart gave a quick throb of fear.

" You promised," she faltered. He sat staring before him, not answering. Then all at once he took the folded cheque from his pocket and threw it almost rudely into her lap amongst the violets.

" I keep my word, even if you do not," he said.

She caught her breath on a quick sigh of intense relief.

"Oh, thank you!" she whispered. She put the cheque safely away in her little handbag, then looked timidly at her husband.

She wanted to be kind to him and to show her gratitude, and yet now she had won her point, now her object was achieved, it seemed more difficult than ever before to stifle her feelings.

Her personality seemed suddenly to be reasserting itself, and to be crying out in bitter resentment against its loss of freedom.

Then, with a tremendous effort, she found her voice.

"I will kiss you now, Roger, if you want me to."

He turned his head and stared at her with sombre eyes.

"Don't make a martyr of yourself for me," he said in a strange voice.

"I'm not. I——" It was in vain that she tried to speak naturally—her words trailed helplessly away, and a silence fell which remained unbroken till the taxicab turned into the Savoy courtyard.

Then followed the strangest lunch Elspeth had ever experienced.

Liqueurs and champagne which she could not drink, and every kind of expensive food which she did not fancy.

" I'm not hungry," was all she could say to excuse herself. " I'm not a bit hungry, and my head aches."

But the more silent she became, the noisier Roger grew.

He talked to the waiter—whom he seemed to know—and bragged about his recently acquired wealth. Elspeth felt her cheeks growing hot and crimson, and her heart beating fast with shame

Why had she married this man ? He was a complete stranger to her, and not even a gentleman, so she told herself in panic, and her mind went round and round like a helpless thing caught in a trap and seeking some way of escape.

She was thankful when the lunch was ended, and appalled at the cost of it. She had never before dreamed that there was wine in the world that cost over two pounds a bottle.

Roger took her arm as they left the restaurant.

"And now where shall we go?" he asked. He was smoking a big cigar which smelt very "expensive," so Elspeth described its aroma to herself, and his face was flushed. He seemed very good-tempered, too, and was not at all annoyed when she answered his question with a fervent:

"Oh, let us go home!"

"And tell the world what we've done, eh?" he asked jocundly. He laughed. "We shall give them something to talk about, shan't we?"

"They'll be very surprised," she agreed.

"One thing, no one can undo it," Roger said in tones of deep satisfaction.

The rain had stopped when they went out in the street, but it was getting dark rapidly, due, no doubt to the grey, lowering clouds.

"Tell you what,' Roger said suddenly, when they were in the train again, "we'll pack up and go somewhere where the sun is shining for a month or two, shall we ? "

" Just—just we two ? " she asked.

" Do people generally take chaperones on their honeymoon ? " he laughed.

He put an arm round her.

" I've changed my mind about those kisses," he said, with a queer note in his voice. " I'll have them if each one costs me a thousand pounds."

Elspeth made a little ineffectual resistance, then gave in, though the tears smarted in her eyes, and her only impulse was to beat him off when his lips touched hers, and to cry out :

" I hate you ! I hate you ! "

After a moment he let her go.

" It's no fun kissing an iceberg," he complained. He took up a paper which he had bought just before the train started, and left her alone for the rest of the journey. Elspeth sat very still, looking out at the growing darkness, straining every nerve to keep back the tears that threatened to overflow.

" I'm tired and my head aches," she told

herself desperately. "He means to be kind really. I shall feel all right to-morrow."

But when at last the journey was at an end and they were leaving the quiet little station, the first person they met was Ernest Smithers' mother. She was waiting at the entrance to the booking-office, her face pale and lined with concern. When she saw Elspeth she came quickly forward, only to draw back again when she recognised her companion.

"Does she think I am the devil, escorting you?" Roger Wynne asked savagely.

Elspeth made no answer. She felt miserable and ashamed. This was how everyone in the village would look at her when her marriage to Roger Wynne became known.

She would have hurried on with averted eyes, but Mrs. Smithers spoke her name urgently:

"Elspeth!"

Elspeth stopped, her cheeks crimson, her eyes defiant.

"I'm in a great hurry," she faltered. "I'm late now. I want to get home."

"There is no need for us to waste your time," he began almost rudely. "I can take care of Miss Hetherington."

His mother interrupted quickly.

"Mr. Wynne has been most kind. I think he travelled down from town with Elspeth——"

Roger's face flamed.

"Miss Hetherington and I were married in London this morning," he said loudly.

There was an eloquent silence, then Ernest Smithers took a swift step forward, his hands clenched.

"That is a lie!" he said passionately. Roger Wynne laughed and shrugged his shoulders.

"You have only to ask my wife, if you don't believe me," he said. "Elspeth——"

She broke into tearless sobbing.

"Oh, take me home—just take me home!"

With an effort Ernest Smithers controlled himself, though he was white to the lips.

"I have my car here——"

"Thank you! I can look after my wife without your assistance," Roger answered.

There was an old-fashioned four-wheeler which still plied for hire between the station and the village, and in it he and Elspeth drove back to her father's house.

Elspeth never spoke all the way home. She just lay huddled against Roger's shoulder, her eyes closed, moaning softly.

Roger kept an arm around her, but he made no attempt to speak, or to offer comfort. He had never liked Bob Hetherington, and it would have been difficult to read his thoughts as he sat there, a big, clumsy figure in the cramped old four-wheeler, staring before him.

When they reached the house he almost carried Elspeth into her father's study and put her down as if she had been a child, in a big chair by the fire, then he looked round.

The maid had followed them, crying in an irritating way, and punctuating her crying with loud sniffs.

She had never liked Bob, but after the

manner of her class, she believed that any death was a signal for tears and distress.

Roger Wynne turned on her sharply.

"For heaven's sake stop making that noise! Where is Mr. Hetherington?"

"In his room, sir. He's locked the door, and won't speak to anyone."

Roger strode past her and into the hall.

"We'll soon see about that!" he blustered. He felt out of his element, and angrily unhappy. He had planned things so differently for this day, and he hated tears and a tragedy, as most men hate them.

When he had gone, the little maid, who loved Elspeth as much as she had disliked Bob, went across the room and laid a timid hand on her mistress' shoulder.

"Oh, miss," she whispered sympathetically—"oh, miss, don't take on so!"

Elspeth looked up. Her face was quite colourless, and her eyes dark with tragedy. She felt as if the nightmare day had been ended by the shaking of an ungentle hand, and that now she was feebly struggling to waken, and to face reality again.

"How was it? How did it happen?" she asked faintly.

The girl told her with many tears and broken words.

"I knocked at the door. It was locked, like it was when you went out, and I wanted Mr. Bob to have his breakfast—it was getting so late. But he wouldn't answer or let me in, miss, and then the master came, and he was angry and threatened to break the door down; but that was no good either, and then——"

She shivered and looked away from Elspeth's tragic eyes.

"Then we got frightened—it was all so still inside—not just like an ordinary empty room," she explained with surprising eloquence. "And I ran for the gardener, and he got a ladder and climbed in through the window—"

She hid her face in her hands for a moment, and Elspeth shuddered and closed her eyes.

"And was he—was he—dead, then?" she whispered.

"Dr. Smithers said he had been dead

about three hours," the girl answered in a stifled voice.

Elspeth sat quite still. She was awake now, wide awake to her own tragedy and desolation.

Her sacrifice had been in vain.

She found herself speaking aloud.

"If I had told Bob what I meant to do it would have been all right. If I had only told him he would have been alive now, alive and safe——"

Everything she had done with such excellent intentions seemed to have gone wrong—everything!

"I wish I could die, too," she thought desperately. Roger Wynne came back into the room, and the little maid rose in a panic from her knees beside Elspeth's chair and hurried away with a scared look at Roger.

She knew him by sight, and feared him, even as the Hetherington children had feared him and his father years ago.

Later, in the kitchen, she confided to the cook that she was sure he had brought ill luck to the house.

" He's like the bad giant in the story," she whispered fearfully.

And yet there was a strange gentleness in Roger Wynne's dark face as he bent over his wife and took her hand.

" You can't stay here to-night," he said, " You must let me take you home."

She started up, snatching her hand away as if he had hurt her.

" Of course I must stay—this is my home."

He flushed a little, but his voice was still gentle when he answered her :

" Your home is with me now. You seem to forget that we were married this morning."

She moved backwards, away from him as far as she could, until the book-lined wall of the room stopped her.

" I wish I could forget it ! " she broke out wildly. " I wish I had never seen you ! I might have known that nothing but bad luck could ever come from you ! " She hardly knew what she was saying ; she was almost beside herself with misery. Roger Wynne looked at her silently, making a great effort to control himself. He was desperately

She tried to ward him off with her shaking hands.

"Roger!"

"Do as I tell you!"

She began to sob.

"I can't leave them to-night. Bob——"

He interrupted her brutally.

"Bob was a bigger liar than I am—a thief, too, if it comes to that." His voice was harsh. "You see, I know all about him, and so if you can waste your pity and love on such a blackguard, you can waste some on me!"

She cried out wildly:

"You brute! You brute to say such things when he is dead!"

"Words can't hurt the dead," he answered in a voice of flint; "and it's the living you have to consider now. Put on your coat."

She made a last resistance.

"Where are you going to take me?"

"To Windwhistle."

She laughed hysterically.

"To an ogre's castle with an ogre. I shall

hate you all my life unless you let me stay here to-night!"

"It will not be the first time I have been hated by a woman," Roger Wynne answered. "Now then, are you going to put on your coat, or must I make you?"

Elspeth stood like a statue for yet another moment, then slowly she held out her hand.

"I must obey you, I suppose," she whispered with white lips. "But I will never forgive you as long as I live."

"Time enough to forgive me when I ask you to," Roger Wynne said dryly.

He stood by while she put on her hat and coat, then he opened the door.

"Now then, if you are ready——"

She followed him into the hall, walking as people walk in their sleep, hardly conscious of what she was doing or with whom she was going. Roger opened the front door.

The rain was pouring down again relentlessly, and the sky was dark and unbroken by a single star. For a moment he hesitated. A wave of compunction seemed to flicker across his face, but it was gone instantly.

"What a wedding-day!" he said mockingly. He put a hand through her arm. "At any rate, it can't be more cheerless up at Windwhistle than it was here," he added.

A moment later the door shut behind them.

ROGER WYNNE pushed open the heavy front door of Windwhistle, held it wide for Elspeth to pass through, and then let it fall heavily into place again.

"Welcome home," he said cynically.

Elspeth made no reply. She seemed hardly to have heard what he said. She stood staring round the great, gloomy house with vacant eyes, her breath coming fast with the stiff climb up the hillside.

Roger had not spared her. He had kept his hand under her arm all the way, and sometimes she had almost been forced to run in order to keep pace with his strides.

And now they were "home," as he called it.

Elspeth wanted to laugh. She felt as if by some freakish mistake she had wandered into the pages of a fairy story, as if she had been carried off to a mountain castle by an ogre. She came to herself with a stifled exclamation, as Roger spoke again :

" What are you standing there for ? If you come in, Margaret will show you which is your room."

He went to the foot of the stairs and shouted " Margaret ! " in a voice that seemed to Elspeth's overstrung imagination to go ringing round and round the high ceilings until it disappeared far up above in the faintest echo. After a moment there was a step along the hallway, and the girl Margaret Dorian appeared.

" I want the oak room upstairs got ready," Roger Wynne told her. He spoke as if to a servant. " Light the fire and see it is warm and comfortable. I have brought my wife home."

Elspeth never forgot the expression of Margaret Dorian's face as she stood there. At first she looked utterly blank, as she might have done if Roger had been speaking in a language unknown to her. Then the dark blood swept across her cheeks and brow, and her hands clenched until the knuckles stood out white.

Such tragic eyes stared back at him—tragic eyes in which the shock of the thing he had just told her turned slowly to passionate rage and disbelief.

Roger laughed roughly.

"You heard what I said! Heavens! How fond you women are of wasting time! Get the oak room ready at once—do you hear? And if you've anything to say, you can keep it till another time!" He turned his back on her and took Elspeth by the arm. "Come into the dining-room, and I'll get some food."

Elspeth found her voice with an effort.

"Thank you—I am not hungry."

"Well, I am," he said uncompromisingly. "Anyway, you're cold. Your hands are like ice."

He took her into the room where, a few nights before, she had seen his father lying on the couch, and Elspeth cast a shuddering glance round her into the shadows as if expecting something horrible to be lurking there, waiting to greet her, but the room was empty.

It still looked dark and mysterious, but on the table, in the circle of firelight, a large bowl of white flowers stood out in strange incongruity.

Roger Wynne laughed as he saw her eyes turn to them.

"The only bridal touch in the place—eh?" he said. "Well, I'm sorry there's no better welcome. Take off your hat."

Elspeth began to refuse, then changed her mind. She took off her hat and coat with cold fingers, and laid them down on the empty couch. Then she walked close to the fire and sat down in a big chair standing near.

"A dream—a dream!" she kept saying to herself feverishly, and yet she knew it was no dream.

The gold of her wedding-ring was caught by the glinting firelight, and she found herself staring down at it with curious eyes.

She was married—married to the towering giant behind her—married to a man of whom she knew nothing except that people said he was mad. She felt as if she had crammed a lifetime into the hours of to-day. Her wedding, the shock of her brother's death, and her father's refusal to see her—all passed before her mind as if they were events separated from one another by years instead of by merely an hour or two.

She would never see Bob again—she kept telling herself that. And yet it seemed of no account. Nothing seemed of any account now except that she was cold—deathly cold.

She leaned back in the chair and closed her eyes. She could feel the warmth of the fire on her face, and she knew vaguely that someone—Roger, she supposed—was bending over her. Then everything seemed to gather itself together as if to spring at her, and she knew nothing more.

When she woke again it was to the little, familiar sound of Ham's whimpering whine close beside her, and, only half conscious still, she put out her hand to call him to her.

"Good boy! Here, then!"

How weak her voice was! It was an effort to make any sound at all. What was the matter with her? Why—— She opened her eyes, and that was an effort, too. Her lids felt as if they were weighted with lead, and her head curiously light as if it were floating in space. But Ham was there sure enough, his big mongrel head resting on the counterpane at the foot of the bed, his faithful eyes fixed upon her with their old look of adoration.

"Ham!" She tried to raise herself to reach him, but it was a physical impossibility, and she fell weakly back amongst the pillows.

How enormous the room seemed! Four times the size it had been before she went to bed last night, with a much higher ceiling and dark panelled walls.

For some seconds she lay staring about her vaguely, not understanding where she was. Then suddenly, as memory returned, her heart beat so fast she thought it must suffocate her, and fear took her in its merciless grip.

She was up at Windwhistle, and she was married to Roger Wynne.

She closed her eyes, with a feeling of deadly

faintness. And then, out of the silence into which she seemed to be falling, she heard a voice speaking her name :

" Elspeth ! "

That was a voice she knew, at any rate—a kind, rather unsteady voice—and she gave a sob of relief as she looked up into Ernest Smithers' white face.

" Ernest ! "

Her shaking hand groped until it found his, and he held it fast.

" It's all right, my dear. Nothing to be frightened about. You've been ill—very ill. But you're better now—much better."

She had never heard such tender assurance in his voice before—never seen quite that expression in his eyes. It gave her such a wonderful feeling of safety to know he was with her that for the moment she was content not to question him—content just to lie still and let her frightened heart-beats slow down again.

Ernest was speaking once more :

" You've been very ill, Elspeth. No—lie still and don't worry. You are quite all right now, and there is nothing to be afraid of."

Her eyes asked him a wild question:

"But where am I?"

And Ernest answered quietly, as if it were all the most natural thing in the world:

"You know where you are, don't you? You are up at Windwhistle, in your new home. This is your own room. You are perfectly safe, and everything possible is being done to make you happy and comfortable."

Yes, again it was the assurance in his quiet voice that gave her confidence. Ernest had said it was all right, and so she was sure that it must be. She was too ill yet to worry overmuch; she was only thankful to leave everything in other hands.

She tried to say: "But you won't go away, will you?" but she was asleep before she could be quite sure if the words were ever uttered or what answer Ernest gave to them.

The next time she woke it was to find a nurse, in a white cap and uniform, sitting beside her, sewing busily.

The room was firelit, and there were flowers standing in a vase on an oak chest across the room.

Although she was not conscious of having made a sound, the nurse looked up, and, seeing Elspeth's eyes open, smiled.

"Awake? That's good! You would like some milk to drink?"

Elspeth would have refused, but she was given no time. The milk was brought and held to her lips, and, though she was sure she could not swallow a drop, she drank thirstily.

"And now go to sleep again," she was told. "No, not another word, or I shall leave you alone."

And so life went on for what seemed an eternity of contentment, until one day Elspeth heard herself saying in a voice that sounded surprisingly strong once again:

"I'm quite well enough to talk now. You must let me talk."

So they gave in to her at last, and with extra cushions at the back propping her up, and with strict instructions only to speak very slowly and not to get excited, Elspeth was allowed to ask the questions that had been lying dormant in her brain since the night Roger Wynne brought her home to Windwhistle.

"How long have I been ill?"

"Nearly a month."

"A month!"

That was a bad shock, and seemed quite impossible. How could one live and yet be practically out of the world for a whole month?

There was a long silence. Then:

"And—Roger Wynne?" she whispered.

The nurse smiled reassuringly.

"He is in the house. He will come any time you wish to see him and feel well enough. He has been most wonderful—kindness and consideration itself!"

"Oh!" Elspeth wanted to laugh. Such virtues could not surely belong to a Wynne of Windwhistle.

After a moment she said diffidently:

"I suppose we're still married, aren't we?"

"Oh, yes!"

She stifled a sigh. No use to hope any

longer that it was all just a dream from which some day there would be an awakening. She felt sure that the nurse was smiling at her question, and weak tears of anger filled her eyes.

"I didn't marry him because I wanted to," she said energetically.

The nurse looked up. She was a kind-faced woman with soft, brown eyes.

"Of course not," she said soothingly. But Elspeth knew she was only being humoured, and she went on angrily:

"I married him because I wanted a thousand pounds. I hate him, really, and when I'm well enough I shall leave him." And suddenly the tears overflowed and ran down her cheeks.

The nurse laid her work aside and rose.

"If this is what you do when you are allowed to talk, I shall refuse to answer another question," she said firmly, and wiped the tears from Elspeth's cheeks as if she had been a child.

Elspeth talked no more that day, but there came a morning when she was allowed to sit by the fire in a big chair full of the softest cushions and when Ernest Smithers was to come and have lunch with her.

"Dr. Smithers saved your life," the nurse told her half-a-dozen times before Ernest was due to arrive. "If it were not for Dr. Smithers you would not be here now, Mrs. Wynne."

It was the first time she had called Elspeth by that name, and a wave of crimson flooded the girl's white face. Since the first day of returning convalescence she had never mentioned Roger Wynne, but she realised now that with every passing moment his claim upon her was asserting itself, and the knowledge brought fear. But when Ernest came he brought such a sane, common-sense atmosphere with him into the room that her confidence returned and she smiled as he sat down beside her and took her hand.

"I'm better, Ernest," she told him. "So much better that you've got to tell me everything that has happened and—and what is going to happen when I am well enough to walk about again."

She saw him wince, and felt his hand tighten on hers as he answered:

"There's not a great deal to tell you, my dear. After you left your father's house that night, you remember, I was not quite happy about things, and so in the morning I came up here to Windwhistle."

He glanced at her and quickly away again. "You were very ill. You nearly died."

"I wish I had died!"

He chided her gently.

"That is a foolish thing to say, and ungrateful." He smiled a little. "Well, after a great battle I got my own way. I brought a nurse here, Elspeth—Nurse Farnham, who is with you still—and between us we fought for your life."

"And saved it, Ernest!" Elspeth whispered.

There was a little silence.

"And—father?" she asked.

"He is quite well, and still going on in the same way." Ernest frowned. "If it were not a hard thing to say, I almost believe he is glad to be free of his responsibilities."

Lunch was brought and she made a pretence of eating, but the food seemed to choke her, and her thoughts kept going back to the past, to the days when she and Bob were children together and to those last few days after he came home.

"I could have saved him!" she told herself in an agony of remorse. "If I had only guessed what he meant to do I could have saved him!"

Ernest had been silent for some time, watching her. Then suddenly he said almost apologetically:

"Elspeth, there is someone you have not asked me about yet."

She turned her face away.

"You mean Roger Wynne," she said in a hard voice. "Well, I don't want to hear anything about him, Ernest."

"He is your husband."

She laughed bitterly.

"I married him, if that is what you mean. But as soon as I am well enough I shall go away and never see him again."

"Supposing he will not allow you to do that?"

She turned indignant eyes upon him.

"He cannot prevent me."

"I think he will try, my dear," Ernest Smithers said gently.

There was long silence. Then he went on with an effort:

"I want to tell you, in simple fairness to him, that I consider we have all—all of us down in the village, I mean—misjudged the Wynnes. Since you have been ill, and I have been up here every day, and sometimes two and three times a day, nobody could have been kinder and more generously considerate than Roger Wynne and his father."

"Have they asked you to say this to me?" Elspeth asked, with trembling lips.

He shook his head.

"I cannot imagine either of them asking such a thing of anybody. I have no axe to grind, as you may guess." And once more he looked away from her, bleak pain in his eyes. "But I want you to realise that these people

Ernest took her hand and raised it to his lips.

" Thank you, dear ! And now I must go. I will tell Roger he can come up."

Elspeth lay back amongst her cushions. Her heart-beats were racing unevenly again, and she was trembling.

What had Roger Wynne to say to her? What would he expect of her ? She was his wife, if the empty ceremony of marriage made her his wife, but he was less than nothing to her.

" I must have been mad ! " she told herself tremblingly. " He is just a stranger to me, and I am frightened of him—frightened ! "

The minutes dragged by until she heard steps on the landing outside her door—heavy steps that sounded as if their owner was trying with difficulty to walk quietly. And then there was a gentle tapping at the door.

Elspeth's lips moved, but no words formed themselves ; and the gentle tapping came again, a little more insistently. She found her voice then.

" Come—please come in ! "

Roger Wynne came into his wife's room with a determined stride, and the usual scowl on his dark face which more often than not merely covered a great nervousness.

If Elspeth dreaded this meeting, perhaps he dreaded it just as much. During her illness he had a great deal of time for thought, and his thoughts had not altogether been happy ones. For once in his life he had, as it were, stood on one side and seen himself with the eyes of other people, and the experience had not been pleasant. There had been a stormy scene with his father when the old man heard of his son's marriage.

"Married her!" he thundered. "Old Hetherington's daughter! You must be out of your mind! What's the good of a girl like that to you, I should like to know? And how do you propose to keep her? You'll not have a shilling of my money!"

"Oh yes, I shall!" Roger had answered calmly.

He was used to his father's outbursts, and thoroughly understood them. In a rough sort of way the two men had an affection for one another, and Roger knew quite well that "halves, partner" was an understood thing between them.

But old Wynne continued to scowl.

"You had fifteen hundred out of me a couple of days ago!" he snarled. "What have you done with it?"

"Spent most of it," Roger admitted carelessly. "And I want some more now. My wife's going to have the best I can give her."

"Your wife!" his father sneered. "A little hussy who has no use at all for you, I'll warrant! I suppose she heard about the money—eh?"

"I told her before I asked her to marry me."

"More fool you, then!"

Roger laughed. He was too accustomed to his father's ways to resent them. He was confident that in the long run he could always get his own way.

But following that scene there had been one with Margaret Dorian, less easy to dispose of. Margaret had made no secret of her bitter anger and jealousy. She had, not without cause, grown to look upon Roger Wynne as her own special property. For one thing, she had known him all her life, and the two as children, both lonely and without other companions, had spent most of their childhood together.

Whatever the world might say of Roger Wynne, to Margaret he was everything a man should be. His word was her law, and for years, ever since she was old enough to understand the meaning of love and marriage, she had been happy in the belief that some day Roger would ask her to be his wife. It was she who had helped to foster his intense hatred of all his fellow-creatures; she who, with the desire to keep him solely to herself, had taught him to jeer at the people down in the village, and to exaggerate their antagonism towards himself and his father. His blunt announcement of his marriage to Elspeth Hetherington came as a terrible blow to her. At first she was too dazed to believe it could be true. Then came Elspeth's illness, and Margaret's flat refusal to do anything for her or help to nurse her.

"I'd rather die!" she told Roger, passionately when, in deep distress, he went to her. "You've put her in the place I ought to have had! I could kill her with the greatest pleasure!"

But when he turned to the door she followed, and caught his arm.

"Roger, you're not going like that! After all these years! Look what I've done for you! No other woman would ever have put up with you as I have."

He looked down at her with unrelenting eyes.

"I never asked you to put up with me!" he sneered. "You did it for your own pleasure!"

"You're a brute, and I hate you!" she raved.

He shrugged his shoulders, and she burst into passionate tears.

"You are cruel—cruel! She's nothing to you, and she'll hate you when she knows you as I do. Tell me it's not true, Roger! You haven't really married her! You're just saying it to hurt me!"

"Saying it to hurt you! Why should I want to hurt you?" he demanded impatiently. "Don't be such a little fool! Pull yourself together and come and help me! Elspeth's ill——"

The hot colour rushed to Margaret's beautiful face.

"I hope she dies!" she stormed. "If I had my way I would put her outside and let her die!"

He caught her roughly by the arm.

"If you'll say any more I'll put you outside and be done with it!" he threatened. "Very well, then"—as she cowered away from him—"let's hear no more. Elspeth Hetherington is my wife—do you hear?—and if you want to stay in the house you'll behave yourself!"

But that was not the end of it, if he thought it was.

Margaret persisted in her refusal to go near Elspeth, which was partly what made him amenable to Ernest Smithers' orders.

Ernest was quietly determined.

"If you want your—if you want her to die"—he amended his words, for the word "wife" refused to pass his lips—"you will go your own way and not take my advice. She is very ill, but there need be no cause for alarm if you do as I tell you."

"You're an alarmist—all doctors are!" Roger retorted. But in the end he gave way, and Ernest took over quiet command of the sick-room.

It had been an unhappy task for him. Loving Elspeth as he did, it caused him intolerable pain to know that she was the wife of this bullying, hectoring man, who was yet such an odd mixture of strength and weakness.

It was with the greatest reluctance that Ernest had at last to admit an odd sort of liking for Roger.

"If he'd had a decent upbringing, he'd have been a fine man," he told his mother one day, with a sort of wonderment. "There is something about him——" He broke off, shrugging his shoulders. "I can't explain it, but—well, there it is!"

"You always make allowances for everyone!" Mrs. Smithers said, almost angrily, for she knew just what her son must be feeling, and she found it hard to forgive Elspeth.

"Such a marriage is bound to turn out disastrously!" she declared.

But Ernest was not so sure.

It was Roger who had gone down to Elspeth's home and fetched up the three dogs—Shem, Ham, and Japhet. Ernest met him on the hill one wet afternoon, with the three queer-looking animals on a leash, going up towards Windwhistle.

"Thought my wife would like them," Roger explained gruffly. "Old Hetherington didn't want them, anyway."

So the dogs had gone up to Windwhistle, and as Elspeth grew convalescent Ham was allowed in her room for a few moments at a time, in the hope, so Ernest put it, of rousing her to some interest of what was going on around.

Ham played his part perfectly. It almost seemed as if he knew to what use he was being put, for he would crouch silently against her bed, his big, ugly head resting on a corner of the quilt, his faithful brown eyes fixed on her face, making no sound—just waiting till it should please her to recognise his presence.

Since her recovery he had been constantly in her room, and he was there lying full length beside her chair by the fire when Roger Wynne entered.

Roger shut the door behind him and came slowly forward. He looked bigger and more awkward than ever, and there was a sort of angry helplessness about him when he spoke :

"I hope you are better."

"Much better, thank you!"

There was a tremulous breathlessness in Elspeth's voice, and yet this meeting was not so bad as she had anticipated.

Her husband's obvious nervousness gave her courage, and she smiled as she looked up into his scowling face.

"I shall soon be quite well, and able to go," she said.

He caught up the last words sharply.

"Able to go—you mean, downstairs ?"

It was not what she had meant, but in her helpless state she was too weak to argue with him, and, to avoid answering, she turned the conversation to the dogs.

"It was kind of you to bring them up here for me."

"It's their home now, as well as yours," he answered. He hesitated, then added: "I suppose you've seen that I've had the address on Ham's collar altered—on all their collars ?"

"Altered !" A startled look leapt into her eyes. "Why, what do you mean ?"

Roger's eyes met hers defiantly.

"Windwhistle is their home now—not your father's house."

"Oh !" She looked away from him with a little shivering sense of finality.

Though he said so little he had already made her feel how irrevocably she belonged to

Elspeth shrank away from him, as far as the big chair would allow.

"Then go away!" she sobbed. "Please go away and leave me!"

"Now you are unkind."

"I don't care! Please go away!"

"You seem to forget that we are married."

She looked at him with wet, passionate eyes.

"I wish I could forget it!" she said, her sobbing momentarily checked.

For a moment they held each other's gaze defiantly; then Roger flushed.

"If that's the way you're going to talk," he began, in his old bullying way, "the sooner we come to an understanding the better! Now, look here, I've treated you decently. I gave you that thousand pounds and asked no questions. I—— Oh, good lord!" He pushed back his chair and rose to his feet. "You won't let me behave decently!" he accused her. "I came to see you, meaning to try to make you feel happier, and everything you say makes me angry. A nice sort of cat-and-dog life ours will be at this rate—"

"It won't be any sort of life," she broke in

vehemently; "because I'm not going to live with you!"

"What!"

He caught her wrist so roughly that she cried out.

"Say that again!" he demanded.

"I said that I am not going to live with you. I would rather die than live with you!"

He was white enough now, and his breath came fast.

"You married me of your own free will," he stammered; and then again: "You married me of your own free will."

"I married you because I wanted a thousand pounds, and because there was no other way to get it!" Elspeth retorted.

Her eyes were blazing and her cheeks crimson. The veil of pretence between them was torn utterly away. Any pity or sympathetic understanding she had felt for him was gone. His own clumsy tactlessness had broken the very small link that held them together, and she looked at him with undisguised hatred.

"As soon as I am well enough I shall run away!" she rushed on passionately. "You can't keep me here! I will not stay!"

For a moment he made no reply, then he said quite quietly:

"Will you not? Well, we shall see who is to be master!" And without another word he turned and left her.

He went downstairs and across the dark, shadowy hall to the part of the house where Margaret and her father lived.

The sitting-room they occupied was more cheerful than the rest of the house, for Margaret had a great love of colour, and she had hung up bright curtains, and made cushions out of old bits of cretonne. There were flowers on the table and mantelshelf, too, and Margaret was sitting by the fire working at some gaily striped material. The room formed a pleasing contrast to the one from which Roger had just come, with its constrained atmosphere and air of sickness. He felt out of his element in a sick-room, clumsy and ill at ease. He was glad to get back to the brightness of Margaret's room.

Man-like, he hated weakness and tears, and his lowering expression changed as Margaret turned and looked at him.

She was beautiful, and she loved him, he knew that, and he was sore and dispirited by Elspeth's unveiled dislike. In his resentment he could appreciate the warmer feeling which Margaret showed.

He pushed the door to behind him and went towards her.

"Smithers is not to come to Windwhistle any more—you understand?" he said bluntly.

A queer shutter of thought seemed to flicker through her eyes, but she only said "Yes," as if it were the most ordinary thing to say.

"And the nurse is leaving to-night," Roger Wynne went on.

"Yes." She put down her work now, and rose "Who is to wait on—on the room upstairs, then?" she asked tensely.

Roger hesitated. He knew how this girl hated Elspeth, but in his present mood that hatred seemed rather like a weapon placed in his hand by which he would be able to hurt his wife.

"You will!" he said.

"Why should I wait on her? I hate her!" the girl retorted bitterly.

"You will because I say so," replied Roger Wynne.

Margaret Dorian laughed.

"You are very sure!" she taunted him.

Roger Wynne caught her round the waist, and, bending, carelessly kissed her cheek.

"I am sure! You will do it because I ask you to!"

Her mood changed suddenly. She pulled away from him and covered her face with her hands.

"Oh, do you love me at all?" she appealed.

Roger kissed her again.

"Of course I do!" It was an easy answer to give, and one which he had given before many times without in the least meaning it. "Of course I do!" he said again. "That is, when you're a good girl, and do as I ask you."

He waited a moment, but she did not speak.

" Well, are you going to do as I ask you ? " he urged impatiently.

She caught his hand and raised it to her lips.

" I'd die for you ! " she said passionately.

In spite of his appeal to Elspeth to give her husband another chance, there was nothing but doubt and unhappiness in the heart of Ernest Smithers as he walked away from Windwhistle that afternoon.

Nobody would ever know what he had suffered since he heard of Elspeth's preposterous marriage.

Even though he had always loved her without hope of reward for himself, and had been prepared to see her married to some other luckier man, he had never dreamed that she would sacrifice herself for so quixotic an ideal. And it had been all in vain.

Her brother was dead and she had not even been able to shield his name, in spite of all her affection, for there had been all sorts of ugly stories floating about with regard to him, and in a little place like Whistlebarn gossip lives for a long time.

But after much heart-searching and painful thought, Ernest had decided that the only chance left to the woman he loved by which she might secure some sort of happiness was to reconcile her to the man she had married.

Ernest had spoken the truth when he told her that Roger Wynne had surprised him by his consideration and anxiety to do everything in his power during her illness.

In different circumstances Ernest realised that it might even be possible to like and make a friend of this man, who had always been looked upon as an unmitigated black sheep for no better reason than that his father was supposed to be a drunken wastrel, and that they never made friends with their more saintly neighbours. Smithers had pleaded Roger's cause with simple sincerity while he was with Elspeth, but once away from the grim old house, and walking down the narrow steep path that led back to the village, doubts came crowding back to him.

It seemed terrible to leave her, ill and weak as she was, alone in the big house which, even to him, seemed like an ogre's castle—

terrible that she should be there, without one soul whom she knew or who loved her.

He stopped on the narrow path and looked back at the dark walls of Windwhistle apprehensively.

What had she said to Roger? And how had Roger treated her, he wondered.

He was on the point of retracing his steps when common-sense reasserted itself. After all, she had chosen to marry the man, and Roger would be quite within his rights if he resented any interference and summarily ordered him out of the house.

So he went home, worried and unhappy, to find his mother waiting tea.

"And how is Mrs. Wynne to-day?" she asked, as she kissed him and took his overcoat from his tired shoulders.

She could not find it in her heart to forgive Elspeth. Mrs. Smithers knew well enough that Ernest had always loved the girl, and her mother's pride in her son was hurt and astonished because that love had never been returned.

Since the astounding news of Elspeth's marriage had reached her she invariably spoke of her as "Mrs. Wynne;" it was as if with her marriage Elspeth had suddenly become a stranger, or a mere acquaintance.

"She's better," Ernest said. He sat down in his armchair by the fire, but left his tea to get cold. "She's up to-day for a little while. She ought to get out soon if the weather keeps mild enough."

"It's chilly this afternoon," his mother said.

She watched him with wistful eyes.

Although he was still quite a young man she could see the lines in his kind face and the grey in his hair, and her heart ached for him.

She did not want success or money for herself, but only for him. She believed he was exceptionally clever, and that he only needed a little influence to make a great man of him. She would have been bitterly indignant if anyone had told her that her son was only a very average young man, making quite as much money as his capabilities warranted.

"And do you believe that, when she is well enough to get about, and to realise what she has done, she will ever stay up at Windwhistle with those two unspeakable men?" she asked suddenly, with great bitterness.

Ernest winced.

"Windwhistle is her home now," he answered constrainedly. "And young Roger is not so bad when you get to know him. After all, the marriage was of her own choosing."

"Quixotism," his mother declared. "Mrs. Wynne must have been mad. Poor girl, she will pay dearly for her foolishness."

"I hope not."

Ernest left his tea untouched, and, rising, went over to the window. Through the gathering evening shadows he could see a light in one of the windows high up at Windwhistle, and again a sense of foreboding shook him.

He wished he had not left Elspeth, and yet—how could he have stayed?

"Have you got to go out again,

dear?" Mrs. Smithers asked, watching him anxiously.

"I must—there are two visits I have to pay over at Little Holden but I shan't be late home."

"You haven't touched your tea, Ernest," she reproached him.

He came back to the table and smiled at her anxious face.

"You spoil me! I'm not thirsty, but, well——" He drank his tea, put the cup down, and, going round to his mother, kissed her. "I shan't be late home," he said again.

But when, an hour or so later, he was on his way back from Little Holden, he was conscious once more of a new, strange anxiety about Elspeth. If only he could see her again for a moment and reassure himself!

He was searching in his mind for some excuse that would take him up to Windwhistle again that night when he was conscious of running steps along the road behind him, and then of someone calling his name.

He stopped and turned, to find the nurse

who had been with Elspeth during the weeks of her illness hurrying after him.

She was breathless and distressed, and his heart leapt in quick fear as he broke out :

" Elspeth—Mrs. Wynne—there is nothing the matter ? "

She shook her head ; it was some moments before she could find her voice.

" There is nothing the matter, if you mean is she worse, Dr. Smithers," she said indignantly. " But there is something the matter because I have been turned out. Mr. Wynne met me at the door when I came in from a walk at tea-time and told me my services were no longer required. He would not even allow me to see Mrs. Wynne again. I had to go to my room and pack at once."

Her voice was full of indignation.

" There was no help for it ! " she went on helplessly. " He sent for a cab from the village, and paid what was due to me, and here I am ! "

She finished in a lost sort of way, as if

she could not really believe such an indignity had happened to her.

"But surely Wynne gave some reason? No sane man behaves in such a fashion," Smithers protested agitatedly.

The nurse laughed.

"Is he sane?" she queried darkly. "I have very strong doubts on the subject myself."

It was not the truth. She had rather liked Roger Wynne until the moment when he met her at the door and curtly told her she was no longer required.

"And, anyway, Mrs. Wynne is not in a fit state to be left," she went on energetically. "I begged him to allow me to see her, but he would not. She did not wish to see me. he said, and he intended nursing her himself. A fine sort of nursing it will be! Between them he and that girl who lives in the house will kill her."

Ernest turned on his heel.

"I will go and see him at once. There must be some explanation."

"If there is he will not give it to you,"

she answered flatly. "And my opinion is that you will find the doors of Windwhistle shut in your face as well, doctor."

He hesitated.

"And what are you going to do?" he asked.

She shrugged her shoulders.

"I am staying with friends in the village for to-night, and if I am not to go back to my patient—well, there is no more to be said."

"I will go to Windwhistle at once. Wynne will see me, I am sure."

But in spite of his confident words, Ernest was filled with doubt as, for the second time that day, he climbed the steep path to the grim old house.

Supposing Roger refused to see him—even refused to allow him over the threshold?

He tried to drive the thought away. Possibly the nurse had annoyed him, he argued. Women were not always tactful, and Roger Wynne was a difficult man.

He rang the old-fashioned bell, and heard

it go clanging hollowly through the house, and then unbroken silence followed.

He waited patiently for some moments, then rang again, and in reply heard footsteps—heavy footsteps—crossing the hall. And presently the door was opened by Roger Wynne himself.

Ernest Smithers tried to speak as if nothing had happened.

"Good evening! I just thought I would like to see Mrs. Wynne is none the worse for——"

Roger cut in bluntly:

"She is none the worse. Why should she be? And, anyway, you can't see her."

There was an eloquent pause, which Ernest broke with an effort.

"My dear fellow, surely——"

Roger cut in again roughly.

"You've seen that nurse, of course—you can't bluff me—and she's told you that I turned her out of the house. Well, so I did. I don't want any more interference from you or any of your friends. You've been trying to set my wife against me. I know that.

And I can manage my own affairs for the future. If you like to send your bill in it will be paid, but I don't want to see you any more."

Ernest was white to the lips, but he kept his self-control.

"Come, come! Don't be so absurd!" he said, trying to speak jokingly. "What has the nurse done? If she's annoyed you, I'm sorry. But you can't blame me for that."

"I'm not blaming you. I just don't want you to come here again."

There was a little silence, which the doctor broke.

"And if I refuse to stay away?"

Roger laughed.

"I don't see how you can get in unless I admit you. How do you propose to set about it? Are you going to bring storm troops and bomb the place?" he jeered.

"You're talking nonsense," Ernest said angrily. "Your wife is ill, and she is a friend of mine."

"You mean that you're in love with

her!" Roger taunted him. "I know that well enough. I've always known it. And I was a fool to let you come to the house at all. Anyway, it's done with now. I can look after my wife without your help. I'm sorry you had the trouble of climbing up from the village again," he added cynically, "but you did it for your own pleasure." And before Ernest could speak or make further protest Roger had stepped back into the dark hall and slammed the heavy door in his face.

Ernest stood for some time in the darkness, his heart beating fast with dread and his hands clenched.

He realised the hopelessness of his position; knew that it was impossible to do anything. As Roger had taunted him, how could he possibly break into the house? After all, Roger was entirely within his rights. He was master in his own house.

He went back to the village with dragging steps. He could not rid himself of the fear that Elspeth was not being kindly treated.

After all, there was a great deal of the

brute in the man she had married, and if there was no love between them—— He could not bear to think along these lines.

It was late when he reached home, but his mother was waiting up for him.

"Is anything the matter?" she asked anxiously, when she saw the strained pallor of his face.

Ernest shook his head.

"No. At least Wynne has quarrelled with the nurse I sent up for Elspeth, and has turned her out of the house."

"Turned her out? He must be mad!"

Ernest laughed drearily.

"He can do as he likes, I suppose."

"Have you seen him?"

"Yes."

"What did you say?"

"He would not give an explanation."

Mrs. Smithers looked indignant.

"I suppose he will be turning you out next," she said wrathfully.

Ernest turned away.

"He's done that already," he said heavily.

His mother gave a little cry.

"Turned you out? How did he dare! There are not many men who would have gone to his house at all after the way he has always behaved. You saved Elspeth's life. Perhaps he has forgotten that." In her indignation she forgot to say "Mrs. Wynne." "There is no gratitude in the world," she declared passionately. "If I were you I would put the police on to him. The next thing we shall hear will be that he has murdered his wife."

Ernest walked out of the room. He was worried to death, and more unhappy than he had ever been. Since her illness he had grown to realise how deeply he loved Elspeth, and it tormented him to think that perhaps she was frightened and unhappy, and that he was helpless to go to her or help her. In the morning he wrote to Roger Wynne and sent the letter up by hand. It was a straightforward manly note, in which he implored to be allowed to continue his visits until such time as Elspeth would be well again.

"Let me assure you that it is my last

wish to interfere in any of your private affairs. I had hoped that we were to be friends."

He told his messenger to wait for an answer. But when, after an hour, the boy returned, he was empty-handed.

"Did you see Mr. Wynne himself?" Smithers asked, trying to hide his deep anxiety.

The boy grinned and nodded.

"I saw Mr. Roger. He said that there weren't any answer.

"But he read my letter?"

"Oh, yes, he read it."

"Did he say anything else?"

"Nothing, sir. He just shut the door in my face."

So that was that. But Ernest was not defeated yet. During the day he went round to Elspeth's father, and was refused admission.

"I mean to see Mr. Hetherington if I wait all day," he told the woman who opened the door to him.

She looked scared.

"That was what Mr. Hetherington told me to say, sir," she faltered.

"Very well, then go back and tell him what I say," Ernest answered obstinately.

In the end he gained his point and was shown into his study, where Elspeth's father greeted him irritably.

"I call it an impertinent intrusion," he began.

"You can call it what you like," Ernest interrupted. "But I meant to see you if I had to stand on your doorstep for the rest of my life."

The old man frowned, but there was a glimmering smile in his eyes.

"Well, and now you're here, what do you want?" he demanded more affably.

"Things are not as they should be up at Windwhistle. Elspeth——"

"Elspeth has made her bed and she can lie on it," the old man interrupted ruthlessly. "If she hadn't been a fool she would never have married that young blackguard."

"She did it for her brother's sake."

"She did it for fiddlesticks!" Old

Hetherington answered testily. "And, anyway, I don't want to hear about her. I've washed my hands of both my children. They've both bitterly disappointed me. One was a rogue, and the other——"

"You are speaking of your own children, sir!"

The old man looked slightly abashed, but after a moment he broke out again irritably.

"Well, what do you want me to do? Why have you come to bother me? I never get any peace."

"I want you to go to Windwhistle and insist upon seeing your daughter."

"I go to Windwhistle? Nothing on earth would induce me to do such a thing!"

"But, sir——"

Mr. Hetherington waved a hand.

"You need say no more. My mind is made up. I will not go to Windwhistle, and I have no wish to see my daughter. She has mapped out her own life and she must abide by it. And now, if you'll kindly leave me to finish my work——"

Ernest could see that further argument was useless.

"If anything happens to her——" he said, with white lips.

"If anything happens to her she will only have herself to thank," Elspeth's father answered indifferently.

He turned his back on Ernest and took up a book.

WHEN Elspeth realised what had happened, her first feeling was one of absolute fear.

If she had been well and strong, she would have been able to face the situation calmly; but in her weak state everything became exaggerated and distorted.

After Roger had left the room she rested for some time with closed eyes, listening anxiously for the sound of the nurse's footsteps.

She was never left alone for long, but when the time dragged by and still the silence of the big house remained unbroken, she grew apprehensive.

It had grown dark so quickly, and the wind seemed to have risen and was whistling round the thick walls of the old house in melancholy fashion. The fire in her room was burning low, too, and she felt chilly.

Once she stretched out a hand to ring the

bell, then drew it back with a little shiver. The bells of Windwhistle went clanging away through the high empty rooms hollowly, adding to the sense of dreary depression which already seemed to reign there supreme.

She raised herself against the pillows of her chair, and looked towards the door. So far she had only managed to walk a few feeble steps at a time, always assisted by someone; she was afraid she could not drag herself any distance alone.

But the darkness grew, and at last in sheer desperation she put her feet to the ground, and by clutching hold of chairs and tables as she went, she at last reached the door.

She was trembling from head to foot then, and her heart was beating fast; but she gathered her strength together, and took hold of the big oak door-handle, turning it desperately.

But it would not open. Half a dozen times she tried, only to meet with resistance. Then the truth came home to her. Roger had kept his word and made her a prisoner.

For a moment she felt that she would die. She slipped down on to the floor helplessly. Then common-sense asserted itself.

It was absurd of her to be so panic-stricken. Nobody—not even a Wynne of Windwhistle—could be such an inhuman brute as to leave a sick girl alone, and in the darkness.

Something warm and soft touched her hand—then Ham's wet, anxious nose was poked against her face.

She turned with a little sob of thankfulness and clasped her arms round the dog's neck. She still had one faithful friend, at all events.

Presently she dragged herself back to the fire. With a great effort she managed to put on more wood from a big basket standing in a corner. The dying flames leapt up and added cheeriness to the room, driving away some of the shadows.

Elspeth went back to her chair, Ham crouching faithfully beside her. And presently she dozed off into fitful sleep, which was broken by the opening of the door.

She started up, her heart beating fast, only with difficulty keeping back a cry as she recognised her husband.

He carried a lighted lamp, which he set down on the table, then he jerked the curtains across the window.

"I'm sorry to have been so long," he said gruffly. "Your friend Smithers has been up, wasting my time——"

So Ernest had not forgotten her. She was conscious of a sudden warmth about her heart. Ernest would never forget her. She had at least one friend outside her prison walls.

"And I had to send the nurse packing," Roger went on. He looked down at Elspeth with defiant eyes. "You're well enough to do without her now," he challenged her.

"Yes," Elspeth agreed quietly.

He gave a short laugh.

"Come to your senses, eh?" he asked abruptly. "Or is this just some more of your artfulness?"

His eyes fell on the dog, crouching by Elspeth's chair.

"It's time that brute went downstairs," he said sharply. He stooped as if to catch Ham by the collar, but the dog growled threateningly and showed his teeth.

Roger flushed crimson.

"Oh, you would, would you?" he said furiously.

He caught up the poker which lay in a corner of the hearth. Elspeth screamed, and with sudden surprising strength, flung herself upon her husband, clutching at his arm.

"Roger—Roger! Don't hurt him—don't! If you hurt him I'll never forgive you or forget it as long as I live."

There was a moment of inaction, then Roger let the poker fall with a clatter.

"I wasn't going to hurt him. I only meant to frighten him. Here, stop crying! You'll make yourself worse again." For Elspeth was sobbing her heart out now, and shaking from head to foot.

"I'm so frightened! I'm so frightened!" she said over and over again like a child.

Roger Wynne put an arm round her, and carrying her over to the bed, laid her down on it with surprising gentleness.

"You little fool!" he said. "What have you got to be frightened of? Do you think I'd let anyone hurt you?"

She flung up an arm to hide her face.

"It's you I'm afraid of—it's you," she wailed.

"Me!"

He turned abruptly away, and stood for a moment looking down into the fire.

"I'm a brute," he said presently. "I'm not fit to speak to a girl like you. I meant to be so different. It's your own fault. You drove me half mad this afternoon when you said that you did not mean to stay with me." He turned and looked at her from beneath his lowering brows. "Do you still mean it?" he demanded.

She lay quiet for a moment, then she took her arm away from her eyes and looked at him.

"If you say I've got to stay here, I suppose

Her eyes met his.

"I want to," she answered.

His face twisted into a sarcastic smile.

"You think when you are well you will be able to get away from me. Is that it ?"

She made no reply, and he went on :

"Well, you won't! You'll never get away from me as long as I live !"

He shifted his position a little so as to see her face more easily.

"Now, look here. There's no need for you to be afraid of me," he said quietly. "All you've got to do is to get well and strong, and then we'll talk. The nurse has gone and Smithers isn't coming here any more. You're well enough to do without a doctor and rotten medicines."

Elspeth flushed.

"Ernest saved my life !" she protested.

Her husband scowled.

"Well, perhaps he did," he admitted reluctantly, "and he'll get paid for that. Anyway I've told him he's not coming here any more. Margaret will wait upon you——"

Elspeth gave a little cry.

"I don't want her near me. I hate her!"

"She doesn't love you, either," he said, with a short laugh. "But she does as I tell her. She'll wait on you, and as soon as you are well enough to be moved I'm going to take you away."

"Away—from Windwhistle?" she breathed.

His old frown came again.

"You don't like it?" he questioned.

Elspeth shook her head.

"It's like a haunted castle!" she whispered.

"And I'm the ogre, eh?" he asked, with a sort of dreary mirth. He looked at her with searching eyes. "Well, anyway, you're the fairy princess," he said. And before she could move or turn her head away he had bent and kissed her.

"And a great many men wouldn't have waited as long as I have to kiss their own wife," he said, and getting up, walked out of the room, closing the door gently behind him.

Elspeth lay very still, with closed eyes. She was trying so hard to hate him.

She told herself that he was horrible; that she dreaded the sound of his step and his voice; that she wished she could die; that as soon as she was well enough she would find some way of getting out of the house, and then she would never come back or see him again. And yet deep down in her heart was a vague consciousness that he had tried to be kind to her and that he had done his best for her.

She put up her hand and touched the cheek he had kissed.

A gentle kiss it had been—a surprisingly gentle kiss for such a rough, uncouth man.

She turned over and hid her face in the pillow.

"I hate him!" she told herself again. "I hate him! I wish he was dead!"

THE days passed away more quickly than Elspeth had expected. The weather improved and sunshine shone in at the window on most mornings, driving away much of the gloom of her surroundings. Ham still stayed with her, and Roger raised no more objections. Every day from the window Elspeth saw her husband go down the winding path to the village, with Shem and Japhet at his heels, and, to her amazement, both the dogs seemed quite happy and contented. She could almost have found it in her heart to wish that they appeared cowed or ill-treated, but they were undoubtedly friendly towards their new master; and sometimes she heard them barking excitedly from the stable yard, and knew that Roger was on his way to unchain them.

He came to see her every morning and evening, only staying a few moments, and always asking her if she felt better and if there was anything she wanted.

One day he brought her some flowers—big, shaggy chrysanthemums, bunched clumsily together with yellow bracken.

"Oh, how lovely!" Elspeth said involuntarily when she saw them. She held out eager hands for them.

"Do you like flowers?" he asked bluntly. "If so, I'll bring some every day."

A faint eagerness in his voice drove her back on herself again.

"I don't want anything," she answered.

She was sorry afterwards, not for hurting his feelings, but because by her tactlessness she felt that she had lost ground with him, and lately she had done her best to be conciliating.

Even to Margaret Dorian she had been almost friendly and kind, although she knew that Margaret hated her. Sometimes she would find the girl's dark eyes fixed upon her with a strange expression in them that made her shiver; sometimes she would feel intensely sorry for her and long to say so.

But Margaret never spoke of herself or of her own affairs. She came and went as an ordinary maid might have done, bringing food and cleaning out the room and fetching and carrying, for the most part in silence.

Then one night she woke up with a strange feeling that someone was in the room with her.

Hardly daring to breathe, she raised herself noiselessly from the pillow and tried to peer into the darkness around her.

The fire was only a dull red glow in the grate now, casting no light, and Elspeth put out a shaking hand to grope for matches.

She was much better than she had been a week ago, but she was conscious of an appalling sense of weakness and fear as she strained every nerve to sense that unseen presence in the dark room.

Then suddenly her hand closed on the matchbox, and she managed to strike a light—a wavering light, very feeble in the big room, and yet strong enough to show her for a second the dark eyes and white face of Margaret Dorian, close beside her.

Elspeth gave a startled cry.

"What are you doing. Why are you here?"

She heard the girl catch her breath.

"I thought you called me. I am sure you called me. Or was it in your sleep?"

Elspeth's heart was racing with nameless fear.

"I must have been asleep and dreaming," she forced herself to say.

"Well, if you're all right I'll go," Margaret replied.

But when she had gone Elspeth lit the candle and sat up in bed till daylight came. She did not believe what Margaret had said.

Margaret hated her, she knew, and she knew why. It was because of Roger Wynne.

In the morning when Roger came to pay his usual visit, Elspeth summoned all her courage and told him what had happened.

Her eyes dilated as she spoke, and her voice shook.

"What did she say when you spoke to her?" he asked.

"That she thought I called to her. But I did not—indeed I did not!" Elspeth protested.

He walked over to the window and stood for a moment looking out at the bright sunshine. And Elspeth said again:

"She hates me, I know. She has always hated me!"

He turned round smiling rather cynically:

"Nonsense! Why should she hate you?" he asked.

"Because she loves you!" Elspeth said.

She saw the dull flush that rose to his face, and his eyes wavered.

"And you do not. Is that it?" he asked, as he came back and stood beside her.

"I never pretended to love you," she said.

"No." He took one of her hands—the one that wore his wedding-ring—and looked at it silently for a moment. Then he let it go again. "You will some day," he told her quietly. "One day you will love me."

"Shall I?" Elspeth laughed mockingly. "You are very sure!"

"Quite sure," he agreed confidently.

She flushed indignantly.

"And when that day comes you will know, of course!" she taunted him. "I suppose your wonderful instinct will tell you?"

"No," he answered quietly. "You will tell me yourself!"

When Roger left his wife's room he went straight downstairs to look for Margaret Dorian.

He was the type of man who did not know the meaning of the word tact, so he went straight to his point with uncompromising bluntness.

"What were you doing in my wife's room last night?"

Margaret turned round and looked at him with burning eyes.

"What do you mean? I'm supposed to wait on her. She called out, so I went to see what was the matter." Her lips curled into a sneering smile "Nothing I do seems to be right now. When I refused to wait on her you forced me to, and now I do as you wish you are not satisfied. I'm sick of you all. I——"

Roger caught her roughly by the arm.

"That will do. I know you pretty well, remember, and I don't believe half you say. Elspeth did not call out, and, anyway, why didn't you take a light? She says you were close beside her in the dark. Done deliberately to frighten her, I suppose."

Her dark eyes met his in passionate defiance.

"You can suppose what you like. I'm sick of you! I hate the sight of you!"

Roger laughed.

"You're changing your tune," he said. "And I can't say I'm sorry."

Margaret burst into passionate sobbing.

"You're a brute—a brute! I'll pay you out for it. After the way I've worked for you and loved you——"

Roger turned on his heel.

"Worked for me!" he sneered. "Only to suit yourself! And as for the other"—he looked at her over his shoulder—"you know well enough whose fault that was." And he was gone with a slam of the door.

He went in search of his father, and found the old man cowering over the fire, a huge, huddled figure in the high-ceilinged, dark room where he seemed to spend most of his life. He looked up when his son entered. If there was one person in the world of whom Wynne of Windwhistle stood in the very least in awe, it was his son.

"How's the captive princess to-day?" he asked.

Roger scowled.

"Margaret's been up to her tricks. I don't trust her. She went into Elspeth's room last night in the dark and frightened her. She and her father will have to go I've had enough of them."

The old man chuckled.

"And who do you think you'll get to replace them?" he asked. "Who do you think will come up here and work for us?

Or do you imagine the captive princess will turn to and cook and scrub for you."

He had nicknamed Elspeth the captive princess from the moment when he first heard of her arrival in the house.

If his son's marriage had angered him, it had also given him a fresh source of amusement. He liked to see Roger flush and scowl when he spoke of her. He liked to tease him and prophesy that she would run away from the ogre's castle as soon as she was well enough.

"No woman ever stays with a Wynne unless she's forced to," he would declare. "Look at your mother! Locked doors were the only things that kept her here, as you know."

Roger knew it well enough. It made him ashamed now to remember the life his mother had been forced to lead. As a boy, he had faintly despised her, and thought his father a wonderful man; but in later years, after her death, he had discovered many things which had changed his opinion.

Old Dorian had let fall a thing or two which had opened his eyes to his father's true character, and he knew that during the past few years only rapidly failing health had kept Wynne of Windwhistle from being as great a bully and a tyrant as in the past.

He stood for a moment looking at his father from beneath his scowling brows. Then he broke out gruffly:

"The Wynnes are all brutes—that's what you mean!"

The old man chuckled again, and rubbed his huge hands together, bending nearer to the fire.

"Margaret's the woman you should have married," he said, with a sly glance at his son. "A woman with spirit, not a pink-and-white, namby-pamby girl who is scared to death of you!"

Roger took no notice. He paced up and down the dark room, his hands thrust into his pockets. After a moment he said again:

"Dorian and Margaret can go, all the same."

The old man shrugged his shoulders.

"Please yourself and tell them yourself. I don't intend to."

Roger strode to the door.

"I'll tell them at once," he said.

He went back to the sitting-room and found Margaret with her father. They were talking angrily together in high-pitched voices, which broke off abruptly as he entered.

Dorian came forward at once. He was a very strange-looking man, with a bald head and a brown face as wrinkled as a long-stored apple. He was short and round-shouldered, with extremely long arms, which gave him rather an ape-like appearance, and looking at him one wondered from whom his daughter could have inherited her beauty.

"You want something, sir?" he asked.

It was a strange trait in Dorian's character that no matter how much in his heart he might despise the Wynnes, he was always civility itself to them.

Perhaps for the first time in his life he

allowed the mask to slip from his face when Roger answered abruptly:

"I want to tell you that you can leave Windwhistle as soon as you like—both of you."

For an instant Dorian looked paralysed with amazement. Then his face grew livid and his eyes half closed, as he craned his head forward, staring into Roger's face incredulously.

"Leave! Leave Windwhistle!" he stammered.

"Yes. Both of you."

There was a tragic silence. Then Margaret laughed.

"That's it! Throw us out for the sake of a girl who will leave you as soon as she gets the chance. Throw us out for a girl who hates the sight of you, and who only married you for your money! I know! I know! She told me herself! She asked me to help her get away! She asked me——"

She broke into uncontrollable sobbing, covering her face with her trembling hands

"You are cruel—cruel!" she wailed.

Roger walked out of the room. He went out into the yard, and unfastened Elspeth's dogs. He was conscious of a faintly uncomfortable feeling at heart. He had never liked Dorian; but Margaret—well, she was almost the only woman he had ever known, and she was beautiful. But he realised the impossibility of keeping her in the house now Elspeth was there. He knew how jealous Margaret was, and besides, there was a steadily growing desire in his heart to put the past behind him for ever, and make a fresh start.

With Elspeth as his wife, and with money at his command, surely it would be possible to shake off the shadows that had clung to him all his life, and emerge triumphantly into the sunshine.

He was young, and life lay all before him. He squared his shoulders and held his head high as he walked down the stable-yard, with Shem, Ham and Japhet clamouring round him. Although he would not have admitted it, he was delighted at the way in which the dogs had adopted him as their master, and he had a real affection for the queer trio.

He took them for a walk round the unkempt garden and neglected estate, and then went back to the house.

He did not care to be away too long, now Elspeth was alone. He distrusted Dorian and his daughter entirely, and he knew that his father was too indifferent to care what happened. During the day he went up to his wife's room several times.

"You look much better," he said once, his dark eyes on her face. "We shall be able to get away soon."

It was quite dark when, late in the evening, a knock came on the heavy front door of Windwhistle.

Roger was crossing the hall at the time, and opened the door himself. A lad from the village stood there, looking rather scared. When he saw Roger he held out a note at arm's length.

"For you," he said.

Roger took the note to the lamplight in the

hall, and saw it was addressed to his wife. His first thought was that it was probably from Ernest Smithers, and before he realised what he was doing he had torn the envelope open and was reading the contents. It was from the little maid who had looked after Mr. Hetherington since Elspeth's marriage, and she had written to say that Elspeth's father was ill, and wished to see her that evening.

"Please come, miss"—so the girl had written in her unformed hand—"please come. He keeps asking for you all the time."

Roger hesitated. Elspeth obviously could not go. It was too late for one thing, and whatever time of the day it had been, she was not fit to leave her room, let alone the house.

"Come in and wait," he ordered the boy.

The lad hesitated, shaking his head. He had never been over the threshold of Windwhistle, and was frightened of the many stories of its inmates which he had heard.

But Roger said again impatiently:

"Come in. Do you think I'm going to eat you?"

And then, as the boy still hung back, he caught him by the arm and dragged him in, shutting the door behind him.

"Sit down, you young idiot!" he said. "No one will hurt you. I'll be back in a minute."

It irritated him that he and his home should be vested with such absurdly romantic stories that even the village boy turned pale and shivered at being asked to cross the threshold.

He went up to Elspeth and showed her the letter.

"I'll go down if you would like me to go." he said, when he saw the sudden pallor of her face. "You'll be all right with Ham here. I can get down and back in forty minutes and see for myself what is the matter with your father."

"Oh, would you?" She raised grateful eyes to his face. "You're very kind," she added.

Roger Wynne flushed.

"I wish you really meant it," he said gruffly. But her words lay warm at his heart when, after dismissing the boy, who ran like a startled rabbit into the night as soon as the door was opened, he went down the winding path from Windwhistle to the village below.

It was a very dark night, with a heavy, starless sky, and there was a restless breeze which tossed the arms of the tall trees, and made a haunting, moaning sound round the old house on the hill.

Roger went down to the village as quickly as he could and across to Elspeth's old home. It was late then—nearly ten o'clock—and he was surprised to find the house in total darkness. There was not a light in one of the windows—and surely, if anyone had been ill, there must have been a light in one, he told himself, with a sense of foreboding.

Supposing Elspeth's father was dead?

He walked up the garden path and knocked at the door. There was no reply, and after some wait he rang the bell. He heard it go clanging through the house, and presently there was the sound of a step inside, and someone unfastened the bolt of the door inside.

There was a long fumbling at bolts, and the sound of the striking of a match. It seemed a very long time before the door was opened, and to Roger's amazement, Elspeth's father himself stood there, holding in his hand a candle, which guttered and flickered in the sudden draught which was caused by the opening of the door.

The two men stared at one another for a moment, then Roger laughed.

"I thought you were ill. We had a note from the girl here—she sent a note to Elspeth, asking her to come down and see you. She couldn't come, of course, so I——" He broke off, a sudden suspicion growing in his mind. "Aren't you ill?" he demanded roughly. "Isn't this note——" He fumbled for it in his pocket, then remembered that he had left it with Elspeth.

Old Hetherington laughed.

"Ill! Never better in my life!" he said. "Someone's been having a joke with you. I'm better than I've ever been in my life since I got rid of my family." And he laughed again, as if he were enjoying the joke immensely.

Roger stood staring at him blankly for a moment. Then he turned and ran back down the path to the street. If this was anything to do with Margaret—some deliberate plot to get him out of the way.

His heart pounded against his ribs as he ran, his breath came in laboured gasps of fear and dismay.

He could scarcely breathe in his sudden rush of terror and anxiety. He would never forgive himself if anything happened to Elspeth. Yet what else could it mean, this trickery, who else could have conceived it. With him out of the way the Dorians could work their will with Elspeth, unable, as she was, to defend herself in any way.

The darkness of the night seemed like a living menace pressing around him, holding him back. Once he stumbled and almost fell; once he cannoned into a man at a corner, who stopped him to argue and demand an apology.

Roger swore at him and ran on. He was sure now—sure that the note had been a trap, and he felt sick with apprehension as he realised that already it was more than half an hour since he left Windwhistle. Time enough for anything to happen—anything!

Then suddenly, as he came into the main village street again, he was conscious of a glow in the sky—a glow that seemed to split the darkness as lightning will split a thunder-cloud. Evidently a fire.

Roger looked up inquiringly in the direction from which the glow came, and his heart seemed to stand still.

There was only one house high up on the hill above the village—only one point from which a fire would show with such horrible clearness—Windwhistle!

For a moment he stood like a man turned to stone. Then he rushed on like a madman his hands clenched, his breath coming from between his lips in broken gasps.

The terrible truth came to him suddenly and overwhelmingly.

Windwhistle was on fire—on fire! And Elspeth was there alone in the house, a helpless prisoner.

Lulled by the sound of the wind and the trees outside, and the crackle of the fire in the grate, which Roger had replenished before he left her, Elspeth had dropped into a doze. She was much more at ease and less frightened now that she had unburdened herself of her fears. In spite of his hectoring manner, and strange changes from tenderness almost to brutality, she knew that in his own rough, inconsequent way, her husband had been kind to her.

No doubt, in the past, Margaret and Roger had been a great deal to one another; no doubt, from Margaret's point of view, she had just cause to be jealous of a complete stranger, who had been brought into the house as Roger's wife.

Elspeth was afraid of Margaret, and had known real terror when she woke up to find the girl close beside her in the darkness. She felt far happier and safer now she had told Roger about it. With all his faults, Roger gave one a feeling of confidence and security. He was a strong man as well as a masterful man, and Elspeth felt sure that Margaret would not dare to go against his instructions.

She must have been sleeping for an hour or more when she was awakened by Ham pawing insistently at the bedclothes and whining softly to himself. Half asleep still, Elspeth raised herself on one elbow and spoke to him drowsily.

"All right, old boy—lie down!"

She patted his rough head and lay back, closing her eyes once more. The room was very quiet and warm, lit up by the red glow of the fire.

But Ham would not allow her to fall asleep again. He stood back from the bed a little, thumping the floor with his rope-like tail, waiting an anxious moment, then he lifted up his great mongrel head and howled dismally.

Elspeth started up, wide awake at last.

"Ham, what is it? Why——"

She stared round the room with frightened eyes. Ham had never before howled when he was with her, and she knew the dog well enough to understand that there must be some very good reason now for his evident distress.

Supposing Margaret were somewhere about again, watching her, waiting for the moment which, deep down in her heart, Elspeth had always felt must come?

Roger was out, she knew, and her room was situated in the most modern wing of the house, far away from the other inhabited part. She listened with strained attention, but there was no sound unless one counted a dull sort of muffled roar which she had never heard before.

Elspeth gave a stifled cry. Something was on fire—somewhere something was burning.

She got out of bed, her limbs shaking.

If a log had fallen from the grate on to the carpet—— But no, the fire had burned low and looked only like a red, watching eye in the dark room.

Then suddenly she knew. It was outside

her room, somewhere in the old house, that strange crackling noise.

With trembling hands she groped her way across the room to the door, Ham following eagerly at her heels. There was a smell of burning now—burning wood—a horrid, charring smell, and smoke.

Ham whined anxiously and pawed at his mistress' feet as, with groping, uncertain hands she tried to find the door-handle. She got it at last, and gave a deep sigh of relief. She tried to turn it, using both hands, but it resisted her strongest effort. Then, with an overwhelming sense of horror, she realised the truth—someone had locked the door on the outside.

For a moment she stood as if turned to stone, paralysed with horror as she realised the truth. She was locked in the room alone —far away from the rest of the occupants of the old house, and Windwhistle was on fire!

She beat on the stout sides of the heavy door with frenzied hands; she screamed out her husband's name: "Roger! Roger! Roger!" over and over again, and yet she knew that he was not in the house, and that she could not hope to make him hear.

Presently she was exhausted. She sank down in a little heap on the floor, moaning softly, and Ham crept close to her and whined softly, licking her face and hands with gentle encouragement, as if urging her not to give in yet—urging her to try again.

Elspeth was not by nature a coward, and presently, with a supreme effort, she dragged herself up again and over to the window, tearing back the heavy curtains and tugging at the window fastening.

It was old and rusty, and resisted her efforts to open it, and outside the rising wind howled round the old walls of the house, and the night seemed lit with a dull, red glow.

She felt cold with horror. To die like this —alone! It was an impossible nightmare—a dream of horror from which she must soon awaken or go mad.

Ham howled loudly and began to run round the room, snuffling at the ground with his blunt nose, uttering little cries.

Elspeth caught him by the collar, trying to hold him, but he would not be held. He was a big, powerful animal, and he dragged away from her desperately, as if trying to tell her that even if she had given up hope he had not, and that there must be some way of escape if only they could find it.

The smoke was increasing in volume, and blinding her and choking her lungs. She put her hands to her throat with a horrible sense of suffocation, then suddenly she knew she could hold out no longer—she knew that her senses were failing her, and, with a little, choking cry, she fell forward.

She awoke to the touch of hands on hers, and to the sound of voices, and, with a great effort, she struggled to open her eyes.

She was in bed, in a bright room, with sunshine about her, and the kind face of Mrs. Smithers bending over her.

“ Better, dear ? ” she asked gently.

“ Better ? ” Elspeth tried to collect her thoughts. “ Better ? ” she echoed again, and then : “ Oh, yes, much better ! How kind of you to come and see me ! Did Roger say

She—— Oh, Elspeth, we think she must have died as—as perhaps she wanted you to die ! "

"You mean—in the fire ? "

"Yes—unless she went away first. They cannot find her."

There was a tragic silence. Elspeth closed her eyes. Margaret dead ! With an effort she found her voice :

"I expect she went away. I expect that is what she did." Weak tears ran down her cheeks. "Oh, I don't want her to have died !"

Mrs. Smithers stroked her hand silently.

"Is there anybody else you want to ask about, my dear ? " she said presently.

For a moment the two women looked at one another silently. Then Elspeth said in a whisper :

"You mean Roger ? "

"Yes. He saved your life, you know, dear. He is a very brave man, Elspeth. I cannot bear to think how unjust we have all been to him."

"He was unjust to us, too," Elspeth said. It was not what she wanted to say. Deep down in her heart there was a little thrill of pride that Roger should be called a brave man by this woman, who of them all perhaps, had been the most bitter against him. But there was an agonising self-consciousness also—a queer sense of shame which would not let her say one kind word for her husband, would not let her think one kind thought. After a moment's silence, Mrs. Smithers said gently :

" It would be kind of you to ask to see him, Elspeth."

" To see him ? Oh, I couldn't ! I——" Something in the elder woman's eyes seemed like a rebuke, and she added slowly : " Oh, very well—if you will tell him ! "

Mrs. Smithers went away, and Elspeth lay still with closed eyes. Roger had saved her life. There was an odd sort of contentment in the knowledge. She was glad to hear him called a brave man. She would try to be especially kind to him when he came.

Then she heard his step outside her door, and a moment later it opened and Ham bounded into the room. Such a queer-looking Ham, with singed hair, and reddened eyes that blinked at her as if they hurt very much, and one paw carefully tied up in bandages. Elspeth hardly knew whether to laugh or cry.

"Oh, you poor darling! What have they done to you?"

Then she looked beyond him to her husband.

With one arm in a sling and his head bandaged, he and the dog made a quaint pair, and there was a moment of poignant silence before Roger broke out gruffly:

"We look pretty objects, don't we? Sorry. Neither of us is as bad as we look. Got a bit scorched, that's all. Windwhistle's gone, at all events. You'll be pleased about that."

"Gone? What do you mean?"

"Burnt down. All the best of it, anyway. All the inside. There's just the shell left. They couldn't get the fire-engines up, you see. The path was too steep, and there wasn't a proper supply of water." He laughed shortly. "Yes, Windwhistle's gone," he said again, a hard note of pain in his voice.

"I'm—sorry," Elspeth said helplessly.

He turned round, looking at her with accusing eyes.

"That's not true, so don't trouble to say it," he said bluntly. "You hated the place—called it a prison. I dare say it was a prison to you, but I was fond of it, anyway." His voice sounded defiant. "Well, it's gone," he said again.

There was a short silence, and then Elspeth said tremulously:

"I want to thank you for saving my life."

"Oh, that!" He scowled and shrugged his shoulders. "Any fool could have done that! Nothing to thank me for!"

"My door was locked," Elspeth said.

"I know."

And now he turned his back on her again to hide the sudden unwilling pain in his eyes.

"Of course you think Margaret did it," he said abruptly. "Well, if she did, it was my fault. I treated her badly. I suppose I treat everyone badly. She liked me. I let her think I liked her. You see, she was the only girl I'd ever known till you came along, and she liked me——" He broke off eloquently, to resume again after a moment: "Don't blame her altogether. It was my fault as much as hers. You're disgusted, I suppose. You've got a right to be. I'm not worth a thought from a decent woman like you——"

He broke off jaggedly as if hoping she would speak, but, though she tried, Elspeth could find no words, and for some time the silence of the room remained unbroken.

Then Roger hunched his broad shoulders together and turned round again.

"You'll be all right here," he said. "Smithers will look after you till something can be settled. I like his mother; she's a good sort. Been kind to me." He touched his bandaged arm. "She's dressed this for me almost every hour since last night. Not many women would trouble."

"It hurts?"

"Nothing particular. Ham got it worse than I did."

Hearing his name spoken, Ham looked up at Roger and wagged his tail.

"And what are you going to do?" Elspeth asked, with an effort.

"I'm staying at the inn for the present, with the guv'nor. They seem quite pleased to have us now they know we've got some money. By the way"—he looked at his wife and quickly away again—"when you're better we must have a talk and settle things."

Elspeth moistened her dry lips.

"What do you mean?" she asked.

"Well, if I go abroad—I'm thinking of it—I must see you comfortably settled."

"I'm not to come with you, then?" she asked in a whisper.

Her heart was beating unaccountably fast. It was one thing to defy a man like Roger Wynne and declare that she would not live with him, nor be mastered by him, but it seemed a different story when he no longer wanted her in his life. He made a romantic figure as he stood there, his big frame seeming almost to fill up the little bedroom, his eyes fierce beneath the white bandage which bound his head—the eyes which so carefully avoided hers. And the old pity which she had at first experienced for him came surging back to Elspeth's heart, making her feel as if she were years older than he, and years wiser and more understanding, so that, almost without knowing it, she held out her hand, and said gently:

"Come here, Roger."

It was the first time she had used his Christian name in quite that gentle, friendly voice.

He hesitated and then came a reluctant step closer. Elspeth leaned over and took his hand—such a big, rough hand.

"I should like to be friends with you," she said, the colour flying to her pale face. "I should like to say that I'm sorry if I've misjudged you or—or been unkind."

It cost her a great effort to say so much; but if she had hoped for capitulation from him, she was disappointed. He stood for a moment looking down at her almost with resentment. Then he dragged his hand free.

" That's all right," he said in his old gruff voice. " You haven't been unkind. Hurry up and get well." And he was gone from the room before she could stop him.

Later on, when Mrs. Smithers came back, she found Elspeth sitting on the side of the bed, crying.

" My dear child "—she came forward with a little rush—" he's been unkind to you! And he promised me he would be careful ! " She put her arms round the girl's slim shoulders. " My poor darling—when you've been so ill ! "

Elspeth pushed her impatiently away.

" I'm tired of being ill ! " she said, with a sob. " I want to get up."

" Get up ! Ernest says you must stay in bed for at least another week. After the shock of last night——"

" I don't care what Ernest says ! I'm going to get up ! "

Mrs. Smithers wrung her hands.

" You don't know what you're doing ! You'll make yourself worse ! My poor child, you don't realise the position——"

Elspeth laughed, and wiped the tears from her eyes.

"That's just it," she said—"I do realise it! And please be kind and fetch my clothes."

THE first time Elspeth was strong enough to go out alone, Shem, Ham, and Japhet—a proud bodyguard—accompanied her. The dogs were all mad with excitement.

It was a bright sunny day with a tang of frost in the air, and a freshness that brought the colour to Elspeth's pale cheeks. She knew that there had been a lot of gossip and scandal in the village. She knew that people were making a great deal out of the fact that while she was staying with Mrs. Smithers, Roger Wynne was living down at the inn with his father.

He had not been to see her since that day following the fire and she had not asked for him.

From various sources she had heard that he was making arrangements to go abroad. Windwhistle, so Ernest told her, was damaged beyond repair.

Of her own future she was afraid to

think, but only that morning she had received a letter from a firm of solicitors, acting on behalf of Roger Wynne, informing her that their client had made arrangements to settle half his capital sum upon her, which being carefully invested, etc., etc., would bring her in a steady income for life.

"Mr. Wynne," so the letter concluded, "is shortly going abroad, and is anxious to have this matter settled before his departure." The letter lay in Elspeth's coat pocket as she walked through the village with Shem, Ham, and Japhet, and deliberately turned her steps towards the inn where Roger was staying.

He was out when she got there, and Elspeth sat down rather nervously to await his return.

The dogs arranged themselves on the rug in front of the hearth, three pairs of eyes devotedly fixed on their mistress.

Elspeth waited for some time before she heard a man's step in the narrow passage outside, and a moment later Roger walked into the room. She rose to her feet.

Roger took off his hat and flung it down.

"Anything the matter?" he asked briefly.

She had felt terribly nervous at the thought of this meeting, but now it had actually come about, her pulses had steadied down and she could meet his eyes calmly.

"I hear you are going away," she said.

"Yes—to New Zealand—on Monday week."

Elspeth pointed to Shem, Ham, and Japhet.

"Can we take the dogs?" she asked.

"Take the dogs?" He repeated her question blankly. "What on earth do you mean?"

"Only that I couldn't leave them behind."

She saw the blood beat up into his face and her heart gave a little throb of joy.

"You're not coming," he said almost rudely. "I've made arrangements with a firm of solicitors. You ought to have heard from them to-day."

"I have heard—this morning."

"Well?" He regarded her with suspicion.

"Haven't I been generous enough? Is that the trouble?"

Her blue eyes met his unfalteringly.

"I don't think you've been generous at all," she said. "You might have asked me if I wished to be left behind."

"You said you did. You've told me a dozen times that you would never live with me—that you hated me—that you——"

"I've changed my mind," Elspeth said.

He came a stride nearer to her, his face almost ugly with its conflicting emotions, dawning hope and bitter distrust.

His lips moved but no words came, and for a moment there was unbroken silence. Then Elspeth went forward till she stood so close to him that he could see the little trembling of her lips and the quick beating of a pulse in her throat.

"You said once that some day I should tell you that I loved you—that some day I should ask you to kiss me," she said, almost in a whisper.

"Well?" Roger Wynne clenched his

hands behind his back. Elspeth raised her face till it was quite close to his.

"Well—please kiss me," she said.

For a moment she thought he was going to give in to her, but the next he had drawn himself up with a little rough laugh and turned away.

"Please—look at me!" she said.

He jerked round angrily, and without giving him time to avoid her or push her away, Elspeth stood on tiptoe and kissed his lips.

Then suddenly all her courage fled, and she covered her face with her shaking hands.

Supposing after all she had made a mistake, and he did not want her? She felt that she could have died of shame as she stood there.

Then suddenly she felt the grip of his hands on her arms.

She looked up, her eyes swimming in tears, and Roger Wynne caught her to his heart.

"I love you! I've always loved you! I don't care if it is all lies. I don't care if you are playing some game. I'll have you on any terms rather than not at all. I've never cared for any woman but you. After all, you're my wife—Elspeth."

She put her arms round his neck.

"I'm so glad I'm your wife," she said.

Afterwards she wondered how it had all come about. There had never been one special moment when she had suddenly discovered that she loved him, there had never been one specific incident that had awakened her to the fact that she had never really hated him—that deep down in her heart there had always been something—something that would have kept her to him no matter what had happened.

If it was love, then she supposed she must always have loved him. She gave up trying to explain things either to him or to herself, she just knew that she was happy to be in his arms—happy to be kissed by him.

"I just knew that I couldn't let you go away without me," she said, and then, suddenly remembering: "Roger, we must take the dogs!"

He laughed like a schoolboy.

"Of course we must! I wouldn't leave them behind myself."

"You used to say they were awful mongrels."

"I used to say heaps of things I never really meant."

"And you'll never be unkind to me again?"

He looked gloomy for a moment.

"Will you hate me if I am? It's a lot to promise all at once, but I'll try."

She laid her cheek against his coat with a little confident gesture.

"I could never hate you, no matter what you did. I've tried, but it's always been a failure."

He held her at arm's length, the shadow of suspicion still in his eyes.

"You're not just sorry for me?" he demanded.

"No, on my honour."

But he was not yet satisfied.

"Elspeth, when did you—I mean—when did you first know that you didn't hate me."

She turned her head so he could not see her face.

"I hated it when—Margaret—when I knew that she liked you."

He was silent for a moment, then he bent and kissed her hair.

"I hated it—always—long before the day you came up to Windwhistle—when I knew you went about with Smithers and other men. I always thought of you as the one woman I wanted, but I never dared to hope——"

She broke in laughingly.

"I believe that's a big fib! I believe you made up your mind that some day——"

"Some day—what, my princess?"

"That I should fall in love with the ogre up at Windwhistle!" she teased him.

He kissed her many times till her face was warm and rosy where his lips had been.

"And if you're the princess in the fairy story and I'm the ogre," he said presently, "I suppose now I've married the princess I must reform and turn out a good respectable person after all!"

Elspeth shook her head.

"I should hate you to be *too* respectable."

"What do you want me to be, then?" he asked.

She was silent for a moment, then she drew his head down to her and kissed him. Strange that she had ever been afraid of this man, she was thinking in wonderment, strange that she had ever gone out of her way to avoid him, strange that she had never guessed what heaven it would be to be held in his arms and kissed by him.

"I want you to be just as you are!" she said.

THE END.

REX BEACH—*cont.*

The Crimson Gardenia
Laughing Bill Hyde
Heart of the Sunset
The Net
The Silver Horde
The Iron Trail
Flowing Gold
Big Brother
Oh! Shoot
The Goose Woman

JACK BETHEA

Bed Rock
The Deep Seam

GEORGE A BIRMINGHAM

The Smuggler's Cave
Goodly Pearls
The Major's Niece
Send for Dr. O'Grady
The Grand Duchess
The Gun Runners

JOHAN BOJER

The Power of a Lie

B. M. BOWER

Black Thunder
Meadowlark Basin
The Flying U's Last Stand
Cow Country
Casey Ryan
The Trail of the White Mule
The Eagle's Wing
Lonesome Land
The Bellehelen Mine
Desert Brew

MAX BRAND

Fire Brain
Tiger
Gun Gentlemen
The Guide to Happines
Black Jack
Luck
Fate's Honeymoon
The Garden of Eden
Pride of Tyson
His Third Master
Harrigan

ROY BRIDGES

Dead Men's Gold
The Vats of Tyre

VICTOR BRIDGES

The Man from Nowhere
The Lady of Longacre
Mr. Lyndon at Liberty
The Cruise of the *Scanda*

J. E. BUCKROSE

The Dark Curtain
The Privet Hedge
A Knight Among Ladies

ANTHONY CARLYLE

The Poppy Bowl
Streets of Everywhere

ROBERT W. CHAMBERS

In Secret
The Little Red Foot
The Flaming Jewel
Eris

A. M. CHISHOLM

The Red Heads
The Land of Strong Men
Black Powder Dan
The Land of Big Rivers

Y CHRISTIE

The Girl in the Corner Flat
The Disturbing Kiss
Hearts Afire
The Adventures of Helene
The Eternal Eve
Her Glorious Year
The Forbidden Love
The Whirlwind Lover
The Girl Who Dared
The Garden of Desire

ARRIET T. COMSTOCK

Mam'selle Jo
The Man Thou Gavest
Joyce of the North Woods

AURENCE CLARKE

A Prince of India
The Lady in the Blue Veil

RS. W. K. CLIFFORD

Aunt Anne
A Wild Proxy
A Flash of Summer

. A. CODY

Glen of the High North
Jess of the Rebel Trail
The Trail of the Golden Horn
The Master Revenge
Buffalo Bill's Life Story

ALPH CONNOR

Black Rock
Gwen
The Prospector
The Doctor of Crows Nest
The Sky Pilot
The Settler
The Man from Glengarry
Glengarry Days

RALPH CONNOR—*continued*

Corporal Cameron
The Patrol of the Sun Dance Trail
The Sky Pilot of No Man's Land
To Him that Hath
The Gaspards of Pine Croft
Treading the Winepress

BERNARD CRONIN

Salvage
Bluff Stakes

RIDGWELL CULLUM

The Riddle of Three Way Creek
The Saint of the Speedway
The Candy Man

JAMES OLIVER CURWOOD

The Black Hunter
The Crippled Lady of Peribonka
Nomads of the North
The River's End
The Valley of Silent Men
The Flaming Forest
Swift Lightning
The Country Beyond
Flower of the North
Steele of the Royal Mounted
Ice-Bound Hearts
The Courage of Captain Plum
The Honour of the Big Snows
The Danger Trail
The Last Frontier
A Gentleman of Courage
The Ancient Highway

CHARLES KLEIN
The Music Master

H. H. KNIBBS
Sundown Slim
Ridin' Kid from Powder River
Overland Red

PETER B. KYNE
The Go-Getter and The Three Godfathers (one volume)
The Long Chance
The Valley of the Giants
Cappy Ricks
The Green Pea Pirates
Webster—Man's Man
Kindred of the Dust
Pride of Palomar
Cappy Ricks Retires
Never the Twain Shall Meet
The Enchanted Hill

B. LANCASTER
The Eternal Struggle (The Law Bringers)

WILLIAM LE QUEUX
The Mystery of Mademoiselle
The Chameleon
The Double Shadow
Mysteries of a Great City
The Crystal Claw
Hidden Hands

JOSEPH C. LINCOLN
Rugged Water

JOSEPH LINCOLN
Cy Whittaker's Place
Keziah Coffin
Shavings
Doctor Nye

CAROLINE LOCKHART
The Fighting Shepherdess

DAVID LYALL
The Land of Beulah
Hidden Riches
Love is of the Valley

ROSE MACAULAY
The Lee Shore

J. HARTLEY MANNERS
Peg o' My Heart

GEORGE MARSH
The Whelps of the Wolf
The Valley of Voices

EDISON MARSHALL
Child of the Wild
Shepherds of the Wild
The Snowshoe Trail
The Isle of Retribution
The Sky Line
The Land of Forgotten Men
The Sleeper of the Moonlit Ranges

A. E. W. MASON
At the Villa Rose
The Witness for the Defence
The Turnstile
A Romance of Wastdale
The Summons
The Four Corners of the World
The Winding Stair
The House of the Arrow

MARY MAULE
The Little Knight of the X Bar B
A Prairie-Schooner Princess